FORGET WAT˙
EXIST
by Ma

CW00448735

FORGET WATTPAD, LOVE STORIES EXIST IN REAL LIFE, TOO

First edition. February 22, 2024.

Copyright © 2024 marianne diatta.

ISBN: 979-8224426034

Written by marianne diatta.

AUTHOR'S NOTE

Bismillah, It would appear that authors, publishers and/or rights holders have suffered prejudice. Works are being counterfeited. In others words, books are being republished without the author's consent. But what do we Muslims know about this? The Messenger of Allah, in a hadith reported by Al-Bukhari:"Know that your lives, your property and your reputations must be as sacred to each other as this day,t his month and this city are to you. Let those who are present pass on these words to those who are absent..." In other words, selling the work and effort of others is a crime. It is a crime to distribute illegal copies and thus deprive publishers and authors of their rightful remuneration. And this is opinion adopted by the Islamic Fiqh Academy: "Copyrights or those related to the invention or innovation of a product are protected by Shari'ah.

They may be subject to transactions on the part of those who hold these rights and it is not permitted to violate them. And also: They may not be copied or reproduced without the authorization of the author or the holder of the rights." Dear reader, be careful who and where you buy your book.

By doing so: -You are supporting the author financially and we know how many of us can be in difficulty -You will be sure to have the complete book without anything been removed or altered -You will benefit from Allah's satisfaction because "it is not permissible to appropriate the property of a Muslim except with his approval" and "Allah comes to the aid of the servant as long as he helps his brother" (Muslim). May Allah reward you for your purchase and for your benevolence. I hope you enjoy reading this book insha Allah. Your sister, Marianne

To my Father, you would have been proud of me

To my Mother, my coach number one. Thank you for instilling in me a belief in God.

To my sisters, my faithful friends.

To my kids, all for you. I love you from all my heart, you are my gift, my treasure.

My cousin , you are a strong, beautiful lady and so supportive.

To my Uncle and Aunty, the best couple. Thank you for being there.

Chapter 1

The Search for Happiness

"You marry a woman for one of these four things: for her money, for her kinship, for her beauty, and for her practice of religion. So succeed, poor you, by choosing the one who practices religion".

[reported by al-Bukhârî and Muslim]

Cynthia was sitting on the sofa, her eyes red with tears. Beside her were her two best friends, Solena and Miriam. They had decided to spend the evening together after Cynthia had received a reply from a brother she had met several times during a marriage meeting. Solena had insisted that Cynthia come to her three-bedroom apartment in a working-class area of Paris. On the coffee table in the living room, the girls had put out cups, juice a bottle of water, and some snacks. "And what's the point of saying yes and then saying no? The young woman burst into another sob. She had already used up an entire pack of handkerchiefs. She sniffed loudly. "If he wasn't interested why waste my time?" She had met someone she thought would lead to a marriage. The brother was totally a match for her, and between them, there was a good feeling. They had a lot of affinities and points in common. Like her, he was still a student. In economics, he worked in a restaurant as a waiter. He had many plans for the future and had a vision for the woman she liked. He wanted his wife to be more than a partner, he would be the one he would take care of and share everything with... For a week, she had felt euphoric, soothed by the knowledge that she had finally found HER person. Against all expectations, he ended up telling the matrimonial agency that had enabled them to meet that he wouldn't be going ahead with it because he wasn't ready to get married after all! The problem is that he announced this after they had already done three meetings. The last one was with her parents. Her father had not gone with a dead hand. He had asked the brother difficult questions about his situation, his future projects, his relationship with

1

religion... His father was neither religious nor Muslim. How would he treat his daughter? Did he have French papers? No problem with justice? The casual style was every day? While Cynthia remembered the scene, Solena buried her thoughts. "I think he was scared. And if he was scared, he wasn't serious about it, that's all."

"Exactly! Do not overthinking ! You will find someone better for you, that Allah has destined you incha Allah. At least your parents are open-minded. I have to choose someone from my village." "It's not that bad," replied Solena, laughing. "Are you serious? My mother has already brought me a binder with suitors...chosen by my aunts and their friends." The two girls laughed. Cynthia was always overwhelmed by the situation she was facing. "Girls, girls "Solena stood up to her friends. "I have the solution to cheer us up" "Oh, what is it?" asked Miriam. She and Cynthia stared at Solena. The young woman grabbed the remote, turning on the TV screen. She clicked on a folder called «my Movies» who appeared on the screen. Cynthia got up to turn off the light and moved back to the couch. "What's the movie?" Solena turned to her, looking mysterious. "You will see" On-screen the film began to play. "Aah! Not yet looking for happiness!!" Shouted in unison Cynthia and Miriam, when she saw the intro. «I don't see the connection with marriage».Cynthia banged her forehead. They laughed. "You give us this movie every time we have problems."Solena shrugged her shoulders. "Well, my little one, to see this guy strive to succeed, that's the beauty of the film. He succeeds in the end! And also you insha Allah" "Well, it's my favorite film, you don't understand Will Smith's masterpiece, poor thing". "Yeah okay." Later Solena drove her home. It had been good for Cynthia to see her friends. The religious reminders, their discussions, and the food had lifted her mood. She made her salah, asking Allah to appease her and grant her a better situation than the brother who had rejected her. It has to be said that she had ended up becoming attached to him and had imagined that he was the one. So she was really disgusted. But when she went to bed, it was with a light heart.

Cynthia felt so happy, holding the hand of the man she loved. Her bare feet sank into the warm sand. The landscape around them was almost heavenly. "I feel so good". She looked up at the man beside her. Cynthia felt such comfort, such closeness. She felt she could tell him anything. Suddenly, right in the middle of their conversation, a huge, increasingly deafening beep was heard. In the distance, the waves seemed like an avalanche of blankets threatening to cover them... Cynthia was roused from her dream. Half asleep she realized that she had fallen out of bed, all wrapped up in her sheets and duvet. On the bedside table, the alarm sounded and from the floor, she fumbled until her fingers came into contact with her alarm clock and found the stop button. "I dreamt about him again". This was the second time she had had a dream in which she found herself with this man. When she woke up, she could never remember his face or the topic of their discussion. Solena, her best friend, had told her that she was probably having a premonitory dream in which she saw her future husband. If that was true, she couldn't wait for it to happen. Once she was up, she did her ablutions and prayer. She always took some time to read the Quran revise her surah and make her invocations before starting the day. It was a routine that she had attached to since she had converted to Islam, several years ago. Later, showered and dressed, Cynthia sat down at her kitchen table to enjoy a hot cup of tea. Last week and this week had been a real rollercoaster. She had a meeting with a brother and had been represented by the husband of a friend. She had hoped so much for this special day! Marriage is an adventure into the unknown and often the culmination of a romantic relationship, but in Islam, it is above all half of the religion! She imagined herself married, laughing with her husband, and sharing lots of sweet moments. On this occasion, she had once again made quite a few films for herself. All the brother's questions were centered on his needs. "He expected his wife to be at his service". "Was she motivated to become his wife?" "How many children did she want? Because he was hoping for a big family. Two boys and two girls to start with." ""And did she have lots of friends, did she work?" As he wanted his wife to devote herself to the home in priority, and she had to be available for his mum, who would need help with the shopping and cleaning. The young woman felt more at a job interview than a meeting about marriage. Besides, he practically only talked about himself. "Me, me, me, I" For her, it was definitely a red flag. She'd given him a straight answer: "I'm sure you have a lot of good qualities but I don't want to go further". She had often been criticized for being too demanding. But should she accept anything and everything just because she wanted to get married? No. She didn't think she was too demanding, far from it. It has to be said that, without bragging, she had a good "CV" Masha Allah. Student in religious sciences, and graduated in pastry, once a month, she made free treats for an association helping people in difficulty. She had been looking to get married for two years. She had exhausted her circle of friends. In the beginning, she was offered good profiles, she had the advantage of being young and never married, so the requests were pouring in. They ranged from the very serious to the totally nonsense. Among the proposals she considered special was that of a 50- year-old man an acquaintance had told her about. He was a good match, she was told. He was a teacher in a madrassah and was known as a person of science. He already had two wives. "Why are you saying no?"

He can teach you everything he knows, it's a good compromise and provide you financially, you'll don't have to work anymore". She turned down the offer. Sorry, but she was not looking for a teacher or a sugar daddy. She was young with needs and expectations for her marital life. At 24, she had different expectations of marriage. And she was looking for more than just a financial support... The other proposal had been a brother in Deen in his thirties. He had a flourishing Islamic card business. His only requirement was that his wife stay at home.

Because, he said, he would be there to provide for her. In full. Because he didn't want her in mixed places. She would have to give up her studies. "Even Islamic studies?" she asked. "Yes, he had replied. He will be her teacher." She had given it some thought. But no, it didn't suit her. She wanted the freedom to learn from people other than her husband. The freedom to educate herself and eventually to earn a legitimate living. She could sell her pastries from home, work from home, and continue to use her art to make people happy and fulfilled. For years she had wanted to make a living from this activity, but also to share her knowledge. She needed to evolve, and to do that she would no doubt have to take further classes outside the home. The same would apply if, at a later date, she wanted to give lessons to other women. So, no, she wasn't ready to give all that up. She'd sometimes come up against people who were looking for the equivalent of a cleaning lady with all the benefits, or she'd be turned down because she didn't fit their criteria, which sometimes made sense and sometimes didn't. "How long is your hair, is it straight?" When she'd been asked this question, she'd imagined taking off her veil to show off her curly hair, and the brother would have jumped up shouting "Oh, that's not going to work!", to which she'd retorted "After the shower it's worse!" She had once met a brother who had been described to her as being charismatic. During the meeting, silence had been their 3rd companion. When she asked him questions, it was as if she was pulling things out of him. He seemed bored to be there. "Cynthia had wanted to believe that that day, this man was probably not at the height of his charisma. She finally asked if he knew what the purpose of their meeting was. The brother replied 'yes' without adding anything else. Did he have mental problems? His intermediary ended up asking if they had finished talking. The meeting lasted 15 minutes. As far as her vision of the couple was concerned, she had never felt in tune with the men she had met up to now. She wondered whether most of them saw women and men as partners? whether in bringing up children or in religious

5

matters. What did growing up together mean to them? The answers varied. Sometimes, she had felt like an object. One day, one of them demanded that she show him her hair and legs, provide remixed hadiths as proof. Naturally, she refused. She had tested the 'halal' dating sites. Two of these sites were well known, but many of the men were already married, looking to flirt, and perhaps looking for a second wife. Or single men not looking for a lifelong partner but a one-night stand. Sometimes just frustrated men because of their failures in their research, aggressive and unhappy with their lives. She and Solena, her partner in crime, had paid the price. As they set foot for the first time in the world of applications, they each decided to meet suitors who seemed right for them. Solena was approached in a message by a 34- year-old brother who described himself as a practicing sportsman working for a software company. In his profile, he said that he lived alone and had no worries about taking a wife with children. He added: "It's an Amanah". After a few exchanges, he seemed like the ideal partner. As for Cynthia, her suitor said he was 26, studying medicine and working in a bookshop. "Do my 5 prayers, go to the mosque every Friday". This was a criterion that really motivated the young woman. He liked to read, loved to take a stroll around museums, spending quality time with his family and friends". For Cynthia, it was like something clicked. She wanted to meet him, but not alone. But there was no one available to organize a proper meeting. As a convert, this was a reality she often had to face: finding an intermediary, a wali who was willing to be present at her meetings with her suitors. At first, people - husbands of acquaintances - were keen to help her, but as time went by, she was increasingly turned down. "My husband doesn't have the time"; "Given your situation, try talking to an imam instead"; "Why did you refuse the last brother you met? He was all right. Maybe you're being too difficult, don't you think?" The worst was the judgment. And the abandonment. She'd been resentful. "Aren't the people in our community supposed to help us?" She knew full well that if it had been their own daughter or son, they would have offered their support. In the end, with Allah's permission, these negative thoughts had passed and she had forgiven them. After all, she had to be grateful, and above all, she couldn't always rely on people. But what she could do was find solutions and rely on Allah, who never abandons his creatures. Cynthia had agreed with Miriam and Solena that they would accompany each other when she met them. In public places. The three girls had agreed to come with their friend and stay at another table while she met her suitor in a public place, a halal restaurant in Paris. "For safety's sake, and so that you don't meet him alone," said Solena. This method was really questionable but Cynthia thought it was a good idea... The restaurant in question was located in Chatelêt and had good reviews. They served Vietnamese food. The decor was very inspired by this culture and the place was really classy. The waiters and waitresses all wore traditional dress. Sitting opposite Cynthia, Anis, the brother had not stopped talking to her, complimented her, telling her how pretty she was. But she'd noticed that he'd been too touchy from the start. Putting his hand on the small of her back as they waited for a table to be given to them, she tried to take his hands in hers once they were seated. The young woman was already annoyed.

For her, it was a "red flag". She must have told him repeatedly that she wanted them both to keep their distance. It made her uncomfortable to see that he didn't respect her limits. Nor did it take into account the fact that she was uncomfortable. But above all it gave her an idea of who he was: he was probably used to meeting women. Because he seemed too comfortable touching her. Apart from that, dinner went well. He was handsome and well-mannered, and he pulled out the chair for her before sitting down himself. The last nail in the coffin was when they both talked about religion. First of all, he asked her if he could see her without her veil... in photos. Which she immediately refused. And he had very clear ideas about temporary marriage. "I don't think it's a problem, as long as both parties agree".

Cynthia looked furtively at Solena and Miriam, who had taken a seat at the other end of the restaurant. It was afternoon and the restaurant was crowded. They finished eating, and like a perfect gentleman, the brother paid the bill and then suggested that they continue their outing by going to the cinema. As they walked through the door of the restaurant, he again put his hand on her back, then his arm around her waist. Cynthia pulled away. "It was nice to meet you, Masha Allah, but I think, given our religious differences, it's best if we leave it at that. The brother seemed surprised at first. He put his hand to his beard. "What religious differences?" "I'm not really in favor of temporary marriage or other forms of marriage" The brother was about to argue when suddenly Miriam and Solena, who had also come out of the restaurant but had moved away, called out to their friend, waving at her. "I'm so sorry! I've just seen my friends. Thank you again for today, and may Allah help you in your search!" As she was walking away to join her friends, she heard : "Ameen, you too". "Girls, that would be a big NO for me!" They had spent the rest of the afternoon together, recognizing that it could have been dangerous. "I really don't think you should meet anyone on your own.

What would you have done if he had been insistent? Or attacked you after being rejected?" Miriam was the most reasonable of their group. She was also the one who worried most easily, but Cynthia, like Solena, had to admit that she was also the wisest. As for Solena, she didn't even try to meet her pretendant. "We don't know if he wants to marry me or my children". In his messages, the man became weird, insisting that there were enough bedrooms at his house to accommodate them all when they got married "I don't mind at all." He quickly focused all his questions on his children: "What do they like, what kind of toys do they play with, how many shoes do they wear as clothes?" Solena began to get a bad vibe about him and decided to put a stop to it. As a mother, her aim was always to put the safety of her children first when choosing a husband. And if she didn't feel it, she didn't go any further. Too many bad things were happening these days for her to take it lightly. The three girls had settled down at Miriam's house. Solena was lying on the large bed, Cynthia on the floor. Miriam was sitting in a chair opposite her desk. The room was scrupulously tidy. Everything is in its place. Surprisingly, it even smelled of new furniture or cleaning products, who knows? Cynthia had always admired her friend's impeccable organization. "If you want the baraka of Allah in your search, and above all to be sure that the people you meet are sincere, you must have a wali, a man who will act as an intermediary even if, and especially if, you use applications". Miriam wasn't wrong. But her two friends thought it was easier for her to say that because she didn't have to go through apps. Her whole family was involved in her research. Cynthia's father was not a Muslim. She had no brothers. Her mother was beginning to show a strong interest in Islam, but she couldn't be what we call a wali. Solena had converted, but her family was not Muslims. So for them, although the end doesn't justify the means, it was only natural that they should broaden their field of research. "You know very well I'm not talking about that. Don't you remember the hadith that forbids a woman to isolate herself with a man? "Solena and Cynthia watched their friend get up and take a book from her bookcase. "The book was called 'FIQH as Sunna'. Cynthia knew this book well because the 3 of us were taking the same Islamic Jurisprudence course. This book was a must-have for every Muslim. "Jâbir, may Allah be pleased with him, reports the following hadith: "It is forbidden for anyone to isolate himself with a woman who is not in the presence of one of his close relatives in the prohibited degree (Muharram), otherwise their third, will be Satan." "And Miriam read the second hadith: "The Messenger of Allah, (peace and blessings of Allah be upon him) said: "No man is alone with a woman but the Shaytaan will be the third one present. Unless she is in the presence of a close relative to the prohibited degree." There was silence. Then Solena was the first to say something: "Wow, imagine being chaperoned by

9

the Shaytan. It's really scary". Miriam nodded, "Yes, may Allah preserve us and make our research easy for us, Amine". Following this episode, Cynthia and Solena remove themselves from all the previous applications. And...They tried again when Miriam herself recommended "MyHalallove", which was advertised everywhere and had good reviews. "This app is different from the others, the conversations are supervised by Muslim administrators". At their friend's suggestion, the two girls were surprised: "How do you know about this app? Have you registered?" "Absolutely not. It was a friend of one of my aunts who signed up and spoke very highly of it." Of course, Miriam already had a network that enabled her to avoid the difficulties that she and Solena were experiencing, so... Yes, it was logical that she didn't sign up!

Cynthia had created her profile:

"Young practicing Muslim woman, 22 years old. I am looking for a practicing brother, a future husband who will be my companion in this Dunya and with whom we will encourage each other to reach Paradise insha Allah. I like sushi, I don't do any sport but I occasionally run, especially after the bus, eheh. Also, I'm a student of religious studies and pastry- making". With that, she already had quite a few messages but hadn't uploaded his photo. Despite the untimely adverts from the app asking her to do so. She had taken out a basic package so that she could reply to messages and contact the profiles that interested her. Solena wasn't wrong, the app was well-designed and you could listen to audio descriptions. But above all, it was supervised. She was going to try it out for a while and see. Maybe the app would give her more control. Because over time, she had started to sort out and restrict the "offers" made to her. Before accepting any meeting. Then, she limited the procedures. Cynthia didn't blame any of the solutions she had used to find her soul mate. If it didn't work for her, it had worked for others. All these methods could be really effective and lead to great stories. She and Solena were even thinking of going to events, a sort of speed dating for Muslims. But not just yet... They needed a good break. Especially Cynthia. She had to recover from her last meeting. Forgot completely about Malik. It was a terrible disappointment for Cynthia and she took a long time to get over it. It was this story that brought her full circle. She couldn't understand those brothers who had chosen to remain single. Unfortunately, this situation affected not only the men in the community but also the women. This society programs us to live alone and makes us believe that we can do without love. With all the technology available, and films that make us live out love stories or experience sexuality by substitution, we have alternatives to meet even our most basic needs, so why bother getting married, forming a couple, losing our freedom, and suffering? This kind of thinking has become more than a belief. It leads many people to choose celibacy as a way of life, as the young woman realized. Today, she was discouraged because she didn't ask for anything else than a man who was pious, kind, well-educated, and...well okay the list was probably long but reasonable, nothing extravagant. Her friend Solena had told her: "Don't look for perfection, look for someone who suits you". It was easier said than done. In any case, after all these encounters, she had resigned herself to waiting for her soul mate to fall into her lap. Meeting suitors was exhausting. It was always accompanied by expectations and hopes. And when nothing materialized, there was that feeling of having wasted her time. And Miriam, who also wanted to get married, had also stopped increasing the number of marriage meetings. For her part, it was her family circle who recommended profiles. Cynthia and her friends agreed in principle to let things take their course. "Let's wait and see, the right one will come along at the right time, all these failures aren't failures at all, I think they're hiding a great blessing insha'Allah". Cynthia believed it. This was no time to be depressed. Didn't Allah say that the strong believer is better than the weak believer? She listened to many reminders about the meaning of trials. And how to ensure that invocations are answered. Redoubling her efforts in her religious practice and her relationship with Allah. Prayer is the central point. She also understood that it was good to have standards, but even better to live up to what was asked of you. The qualities and criteria she was looking for in her future husband, she strove to have. After all, you have to look at yourself first, as someone once said! She lay back on the sofa. She had just received a notification. She'd seen a profile of someone called Ilyas. "I'm a very religious 35-year-old brother. I do my 5 prayers. I work in a bookshop. I like sports and spending time with my friends. I don't have any standard perfection about women. For me, the most important thing is that she should be my partner for the satisfaction of Allah. That we laugh together and help each other on a daily basis." Reading the beginning of this profile, Cynthia had sensed that he might be the one. He was old compared to her, but young people his age weren't necessarily mature. She decided to give him a chance and read the message: "Salam, how are you?" "Fine Al Alhamdulillah and you?" she answered. " Alhamdulillah. Where do you live?" The young woman lay back on the sofa to make herself comfortable. "I'm in Paris" "Ok, I'm in Avignon. Would you agree to a long- distance marriage?" "Er...What do you mean?" "You're in Paris, I'm in Avignon". Cynthia rolled over onto her stomach, tapping away on her phone. "Yes, but I don't understand. By distance, do you mean you'd be in Avignon and I'd stay in Paris?" "Yes, that' s right . I'll come and see you every fortnight". "Wow, what's he talking about?" She received another message: "Send me your photo, we'll start there". "My boy, it's dead," thought Cynthia. She typed angrily: "Thanks but no thanks. I'm not interested in polygamy or a long-distance marriage. "And she blocked him. What the hell was that all about? What psychopath??? He didn't even try to get to know me, he just told me about the photo... And suggested a weird plan... " If he'd approached her about polygamy, that was his right - a right in Islam. But she appreciated it when people were transparent about their intentions. Personally, she wasn't interested in polygamy because, for one thing, she felt she still had other options at her age. She didn't have any children either. And secondly, she couldn't imagine managing both a husband AND a first wife. Women can be so jealous of each other. Cynthia had heard of polygamous marriages that hadn't ended well, and psychologically she wasn't ready for that. She had discussed the matter with Solena, who received proposals of this kind all the time, and she too had the same opinion. However, she had finally decided that she could accept if, in addition to religion, the brother in question had a very good financial situation, and was, therefore, able to provide for two families. Cynthia puts a pillow over her face to muffle her angry scream. She immediately deleted the app. She was so upset! "Sorry but "Myhalallove" won't be for me. We're going to avoid another trauma"!

Chapter 2

Travel, Travel

Allah does not require of any soul more than what it can afford. All good will be for its own benefit, and all evil will be to its own loss. ⸢The believers pray,⸣ "Our Lord! Do not punish us if we forget or make a mistake. Our Lord! Do not place a burden on us like the one you placed on those before us. Our Lord! Do not burden us with what we cannot bear. Pardon us, forgive us, and have mercy on us. You are our ⸢only⸣ Guardian. So grant us victory over the disbelieving people."

[Surah Al Baqarah Verse 286]

The next day, Cynthia got ready to go out. She had just put on a dark blue abaya and a new hijab, which she had ordered several weeks earlier. "I like it, really, really nice Masha Allah", she said to herself as she looked in the mirror. This afternoon she was going to join a group of sisters on a trip organised by a Muslim association. She was excited about it. "Finally something exciting. Can't wait to leave," she said to herself. She made her invocations before leaving. As she closed her front door, she bumped into her next- door neighbour, Madame Bakhri, coming towards her. She was an old woman, a Muslim, always smiling and friendly, a good woman. She had two cats. She regularly complained about the upstairs neighbours and knew all the gossip in the building and...Maybe all of Paris, who knows? Every time she cooked, Cynthia could smell the wonderful smells that made her mouth water... Especially when, during exam periods, or when the month's end proved to be a challenge, she sometimes had to make do with fast food or a basic dish. But Madame Bakhri must have had a sixth sense because from time to time she would bring her one of her delicious dishes.

They said salaam to each other and Cynthia rushed down the stairs. Outside, the fresh air on her face did her a world of good. Before the famous trip, she had to make a short stop at her former workplace... and hand in her letter of resignation. The sooner this was done, the better it was. When she arrived at the factory, where all the delicacies for the big hotels and airlines were prepared, all heads turned towards her. She would have liked to photograph their amazed faces. Among the people in her team, there were friendly smiles. The young woman remembered all the times she'd had to take off her veil and put it back on at the end of the day when she left the premises, for a whole year. This time had been a testing period for her. One of her friends, who wears the hijab too, had decided to move to England. "We shouldn't have to take off our veils to study! Why don't you come and live here, or in a Muslim country?" For years, the government had banned veiled women from wearing the veil in institutions such as schools and most companies. Muslims people in France first protested, and a powerful association defended their rights... Their actions were restricted, but as the years went by and laws became tougher and increased, the community eventually adapted, either by accepting the constraints or by finding alternatives (such as studying and working from home). Or wear alternatives to the veil. Even on passports, women in veils or niqabs were obliged to remove their hijab. When she went to England to visit her cousin, she saw that English Muslims were stunned and offended by this situation. Because they had religious freedom. Cynthia had decided to choose the alternatives. At that stage of her life, she still couldn't afford to move. Every penny she earned was scrupulously recorded in a notebook. Sometimes she had to tighten her belt. Despite the desire to leave, she was not yet financially ready. Al Hamdulillah, the headmaster allowed her to wear a bonnet under her cap, with which she wore turtlenecks. For the exams orals, the school allowed her to wear a turban. She knew that a solid background would have been necessary for her to leave this Islamophobic country. How could she settle in a foreign country with no income? She couldn't rely entirely on her family. Firstly, they didn't understand her choice to leave and secondly, they couldn't finance her indefinitely. In the end, she graduated as a pastry chef. She then found a small job as an apprentice in the school "Chocolat & Mignardises* Dargé". It was a reputed place that was in an old area district of Paris. The buildings were full of stories, the streets still imprinted with the past, passers-by, customers enjoying their coffee or reading their newspaper in the cafes and the refined tea salon. Cynthia loved the atmosphere. Then what a joy to be able to work and learn every day in a place that had hosted some of the best pastry chefs in France. For the young woman, this represented an accomplishment in itself and the beginning of a dream in the profession she wanted to integrate. She had loved being part of the team. But she now had other ambitions...Not least that of working for herself. This would allow her to wear her hijab without fear of someone asking her to take it off. It would also make it easier for her to do her prayers on time. It was risky but worth it. Definitely. "Well then, Cynthia, you're late...but I'm not going to "veil" my face from you any longer." His boss's laughter was accompanied by the laughter of some of his colleagues. How happy she was to leave if he only knew! "I've come to hand in my letter of resignation." Replied the young woman. She was nervous but so happy to hand it to him. Just to see his face. After all, she was one of his most valuable assets. And she wasn't wrong, The astonishment she saw from her boss was quickly hidden by one of his insipid jokes. "Where are you going? Afghanistan, Syria?" As her boss laughed with a big laugh, she met the gaze of the man who had precipitated her departure. Samuel, a colleague with whom she had become dangerously close. Although she did everything to protect herself, a friendship and then a strong attraction had developed. Samuel was a Muslim, but like many young people of their generation, he didn't practice. So the young man lived with religious references but was not interested in them. For Cynthia, their "story" could lead nowhere. So she cut it off. No more phone calls, no more late-night discussions, no more exchanging glances. That's when she started meeting people with a view to marriage. Hoping to forget the young man for good by

16

finding someone who would suit her. But Samuel was not someone who gave up easily. Confident of his attractiveness, he had tried everything to rekindle their bond. He had confessed his feelings for her and spared no effort to show them. This day,knowing that she was always the first to arrive at work, he too arrived at the same time to take advantage of their brief moment of solitude and talk to her.

He was always trying to get a smile or a laugh out of her or to come to her help if she was having trouble with her pastry. In the evenings, he would wait for her and offer her a ride home, but she would always decline, come rain or shine. And it was difficult for her. Allah only knew how much she wanted him in her life. She had already imagined all kinds of scenarios where they got together, without any restrictions. She listened to the voice of her passions and the Shaytan whispering to her that it cost her absolutely nothing to spend time with him or phone him, as long as it remained innocent. But Cynthia was determined not to give in to the boy's game of seduction. She had got to know him and even if his feelings seemed sincere, he was absolutely not ready to get married or change his lifestyle. She knew that. "We can't go out together, I want to get married and start a family". "I can offer you all this if you give me a chance...You could teach me how to practice" he used to say. But both he and she knew it was all talk. She knew examples of girls who promised to wear the veil or men who promised to pray and give up their bad habits, but once they were married, these promises were often a thing of the past. You don't just change like that! She knew this all too well. As a revert. Going from a carefree life with a feeling of freedom and not having to answer to anyone... to a life as a Muslim, performing her 5 prayers, abandoning habits and a lifestyle that didn't conform to Islam didn't happen overnight. Giving up what you do and changing who you are must be done with a sincere and pure intention and for Allah. Not to please people or to make ends meet and Samuel was the stubborn type who would only do what suited him. She knew that his promises of change wouldn't last indefinitely, not as long as he didn't practice voluntarily. Long months of playing cat and mouse. In the end, a decision had to be made. And to avoid crossing a line and falling into haram, she had chosen to leave. Not just because of him, but also for herself, to find herself and focus on her goals. The first of which was to be at peace with herself. It was time to look to the future, to grow in her faith, and to fulfill half of her religion insha Allah. Cynthia was positive and not worried about her future. Fate is an unknown thing, but as long as you have faith... One morning, as she was reading the surah Al Qasas, she came across this verse in which Mûsâ ('alayhi salam) made this Dua: "Lord, I am in great need of any grace you will kindly bestow upon me". After that, his situation improved as he found refuge and security as well as a promise of marriage. It had filled Cynthia with hope and since then she had never stopped including the invocation she had just her, her wish. She also had her big sister Amélie, who encouraged her and helped her to stay positive. For many years Amélie had met many great difficulties in getting pregnant. It was only after 5 years that she and her husband finally had their first child. They were a solid couple and had come through this great test together, read in each of her prayers. She knew that sooner or later, Allah would grant which had brought them closer together. She was a real example to Cynthia. She knew that her sister had broken down, but she had always seen her as positive and determined. She wasn't a Muslim but she had always supported her in her choices. "She encouraged her and gave her the best advice a big sister could give. As far as Samuel was concerned, it was Amélie who had advised her first to get it over with and not let things drag on. "You know, once you fall in love, all your reason falls asleep. End it while you still have the strength to make the right decisions for yourself". Her sister knew what she was talking about because before she met her husband, she had experienced great disappointment in love with a man she had known since high school.

He promises to her the moon. Telling her that he wants to marry her after their studies. Then it was "when I find a job", and when he did find a job, other excuses came up. They remained "engaged" for 8 years. Finally, he announced that he wasn't ready to start anything with her. He felt too young to get married. And he wanted to live his own life. Amélie liked to talk about it because years later after she had moved on professionally and emotionally with the man she now shared her life with, she had bumped into this ex-boyfriend again. He had never been able to settle down and had known many women. At 35, he was still so immature. He started flirting with Amélie until she was joined by her husband. "And then you should have seen how his smile dropped". It was an anecdote that made them laugh a lot. So in terms of advice, Amélie definitely had the experience. Cynthia was happy to have been comforted in her decision to distance herself from Samuel. Her friends had also encouraged her. "It is a smooth talker, don't waste your time." So she didn't hesitate, dragging Solena into her travel plans. She didn't know what awaited her, but she was sure of one thing: you must always rely on Allah. He is the best of planners. She said her goodbyes to some of her female colleagues with whom she had good relations, and as she left, Cynthia saw that Samuel was coming towards her. She said goodbye with a quick wave of her hand. And left. Disturbed to have seen him again, but proud and relieved to have found the strength not to go back to him. She wanted so much to talk to him, to ask him if he was all right, to let him hold her... She was already outside hearing her name. She turned and saw Samuel running to her. He wore a hat and a black uniform with the school emblem. "Where are you going?" Cynthia hesitated to answer but in front of Samuel's destabilized look, she replied with a small voice: 'I am leaving for Oman with sisters insha Allah'. Samuel took off his hat, not caring at all for the passers-by who looked at them both with curiosity. Her beautiful short, wavy hair was disheveled. Her slightly neglected and disabused air added to her charm. "I know you 3don't want anything between us, but if you need anything, I'm here. No matter where you go..."

"Anywhere in the world?" asked Cynthia, "Anywhere to you." replied Samuel while putting on his hat, looking at her. "Okay Cycy, have a nice stay. I have to go or else I'll get burned", but instead of leaving, he waited for her to leave. "Salam Samuel", "Salam Cynthia. Call me". "You know I won't." "So at least think of me." the young man added. Cynthia left, unable to help but smile.

She quickly got into the subway, which was crowded as usual. It was still early, and at every station, people were pouring in to get to work. But you could tell it was the school holidays because there were lots of young people and groups of tourists. She'd grown up in this country, in this city, and the racism and Islamophobia that were so prevalent made her want to leave. Dreaming of being somewhere else. She had never been to a Muslim country. Oman will be the first.

Chapter 3

Everything for family

"He looked at her intensely. His qamis accented his steely pecs. He said to her: "Call me Franco babe." The girl took the Quran from his hands, her gaze downcast. Her heart was racing. She could feel the wind on her face, the love singing in her belly, unless it was hunger. Hunger to be with Franco... But she was also really hungry and thought of her mother's rice dish..."

"Close your book, darling! Forget Wattpad, there are real-life love stories too, and I'm sure we'll find our Franco in Oman!!!" Solena shouted hysterically. Cynthia closed the app. The "book" she was reading was in fact an online romance she used to read on wattpad app. It was called "Gone with the Love". It was about a girl who is torn between a rich bad boy heir, Antonio and the nice farmer Franco. What can she say about the story... It really was the worst on Wattpad! The characters were so cartoonish, not to mention the dialogue... But it was her little pleasure. Because it made her laugh and nurtured her cheesy side. She was already too involved in the story and wanted to know which of Franco or Antonio, Astafara would choose. Cynthia laughed, she had become so invested in the online book that she had neglected her luggage. Her clothes were folded and placed on a chair, her toiletry bag was on the floor, and further back she had some shoes. She had spent the night in her room at her parents' house. And of course, first, she had to kick out her 16- year- old little sister, who hadn't hesitated to move in. "I don't know who told you, you could, but you can't. Even if I have 40, 5 kids, and live in Dubai, it will be my room forever." Her sister Eve stormed out of the room. "You never want to share anyway!" Eve was too dramatic. But the next morning, she slipped into the bedroom to say goodbye, give her a big hug, and wish her a safe journey. "Thank you, little sister." Her sister was in her "all-black" phase. Black hair, black makeup, goth clothes. She listened to Black Pink and other bands that only she knew. The arguments for her to lower the sound had got the better of Cynthia's patience. Although it was a long-standing project, it was the breaking point that motivated her to move. Apart from that, her little sister respected her a lot and learned to adapt little by little to Cynthia's transition into Islam. The young woman finished putting her clothes in her bag. She added 2 books and a Quran. Plus her notebook to revise her fiqh lessons. Her mother burst into the room, "Girls, when you've finished, please put your bags in the car. They were so excited! "Who's going to Oman? Who's going to Oman?" Solena pretended to sing in an imaginary mic. "It's us, it's us", replied Cynthia in the same tone both jumped onto the bed. They both burst out laughing. "Add masha Allah" In the midst of their delirium, they do not heard a knock at the door. Miriam entered and interrupted them. "Salam alaykum girls. Well, it's festive here! It's starting to make me regret not leaving with you!" The girls greeted her, "We're going to miss you..." said Solena, taking her in her arms. We'll try not to have too much fun without you." "Thank you for your dedication," Miriam replied ironically. Then she went down on the bed. Are you sure your parents won't let you? Cynthia asked her "Yes! Sure. They need me at the store." Cynthia felt disappointed for her friend. But she understood that the young woman had responsibilities and other priorities. Last year, the country and especially Paris, had been ravaged by social riots. Mobs destroyed shop windows, including that of Miriam's parents. Fortunately, they had insurance, however, in their neighborhood, only their store had been targeted. The police had done the bare minimum in their investigation and quickly closed the case. Her parents were immigrants from Bangladesh but although in France for more than 40 years, Miriam saw that they were still victims of racism or belittled before the authorities or administrations because of their status. But their revenge was that they made a good living. With 2 other groceries stores in Paris, all their children succeeded in school, and above all they were a united family. The shop was quickly put back on its feet thanks to the uncles, cousins, and aunts. However, Miriam's parents had demanded that she be there now to help her mother at the checkout and take turns with one of her cousins. Cynthia kissed her friend. "We will call you once in Oman. Be good in our absence," she added to tease her. I must rather worry about you... » Miriam said with a false serious look. When the young woman left them, Cynthia finish to pack her luggage. Only a few hours left before their trip. "It will be unforgettable insha Allah" The young woman thought to herself. Miriam, went home. On the way, she thought of this trip to Oman. Frankly, in addition to the shop, she also had to revise her courses for the next exams. She would not have had time. Kheir insha Allah. She lived in the family home. It was a large pavilion, modern and located in a residential area. The fruit of her parents' hard work, the house where she was born and raised. «Salam mom» She went straight to her room. She knew that her friends thought life was easy for her and that everything was working for her. No. It wasn't. Of course, the financial aspect was not a problem, but from a very young age, she carried a weight on her shoulders. Too much pressure. Her parents wanted her to excel in her studies because they did not want their daughters to suffer the racism they experienced on a daily basis. "Unfortunately, in this world, people respect you for 2 things: Your status and your money. And if you're pretty, it's a bonus. But it's still not enough. Worked for the first two goals my dear daughter. Work hard." Her mother had never stopped telling her that. She was the favorite child of her father, the youngest of three older brothers and two older sisters. All adults now, they lived in their own homes, in France and England where there were other family members. At the age of 23, Miriam was the only one left in the family home. And every week, she went to their nearby grocery store to help them. For them who had had their daughter practically by surprise, she represented a gift from Allah. And for that, she had always been more spoiled than the others. But suddenly, she felt more pressure not to disappoint her parents. Miriam was enrolled in calligraphy classes, and she also did athletics sport but because of the ban on the hijab, she had to stop. She was still first in her class and had now started studying to become a doctor. She wanted to help the Muslim community. Her phone was vibrating, but she turned it off. She had too much on her mind. And in particular, someone. He said, "I know you. We are in the same University, same course, right?" A difficult secret to keep for the one that everyone considers a good girl and innocent...Reliable. Just last year, when the store had just re-opened after weeks of work, Ousmane had appeared. She knew him from University, although in the same class, they had never spoken to each other...until that famous day. And from there they had begun to speak. She could not help herself because at that moment she was running the store alone and was bored to death. It was summer...and in the summer, people were leaving. If everything went well, she had about ten clients in the day, spaced out over hours. Ousmane was tall, his dark skin, his penetrating and narrow eyes which the young woman had quickly drowned. It was an almost new feeling for her, because of one she had never felt particularly attracted to blacks or boys in general. Her studies and responsibilities took her so much time that she spent more time dreaming of love.

Her ideal was the indian actor Ishaan Khatter or Ahan Shetty...

But here Ousmane with his beautiful smile. He reminded her of the Tuaregs, the men in the desert. He seemed so mysterious, calm, smart and yeah... Ousmane was just amazing Masha Allah.

Yes. Okay. She had met some men through her parents and aunts but it was more of an obligation to satisfy them rather than for her own needs. Also that day, Ousmane had immediately captured his attention because he expressed himself gently and a certain nonchalance that contrasted with the virility that emanated from him. The young man had a friend around, that's what brought him there. He just came to buy Sprite cans. But the next week he came back, one Friday, then the Friday after. He would go to a small prayer room nearby and stop to buy Sprite cans. Gradually, Miriam had developed feelings for him. And a strong attraction. She had caught herself stealing her mother's mascara. And finally bought one. Then, little by little, she started to pay more attention to her outfit. As soon as she left the prayer room, she rushed to the store to be sure not to miss the brother. The two young people could no longer hide their feelings for each other. Ousmane finally confessed it to her first and confided with a charming smile that he did not even like the Sprite but that he had ended up buying it just to be able to see her. And then he asked her if she was thinking of getting married... She said yes and they both laughed embarrassed and at the same time happy to share mutual feelings. Only, Miriam thought of her family... She knew that her parents, more her mother would not agree. And all that... Well, she had not told the girls. Worse, she had not told them that she spoke with the young man by text. She, Miriam, the good girl, always ready to give advice... That she did not follow herself in the end. What would be her limit? So ashamed, she didn't know when to talk about it and where to start. And then her two friends left... Ousmane wanted to come to her home to ask her parents for her hand. The situation stressed her so much! Her parents were rather old-fashioned and she knew that it would be difficult to make them accept a stranger when they dreamed of seeing her marry someone from the country.

She sighed and sat on her bed, grabbed the remote, and turned on the TV screen. «Red Flags» from Kimberley Show, was about to start. On the screen, we see a young blonde woman, hair impeccably styled, dressed, and manicured. "Today we welcome guests who had everything to succeed but abandoned everything for love. Why?! How? Did they not see the signs that their man duped them?" As a result, their relationship ended like the Titanic." With a dramatic face, she raised her hands and snapped her fingers and was followed by the crowd. «I am Kimberly Show and you are on the show set of Red Flaaaags» Miriam sighed.

"I preferred when she presented "blind to first love."

Chapter 4

Looking for a pious and practising Brother

The Prophet (ﷺ) said: "Two whispers arise in the heart, the first coming from the angel arousing the good and the will to believe in the truth, let him who feels it know that it comes from Allah, may He Praise Him; and the second, coming from the enemy (Satan) arousing evil and the will to deny the truth and turn away from the good, let him who feels it seek help from Allah against Satan the accursed." [**Reported by Tirmidhî, fairly authentic hadith (Hassan]**

Lying back on the sun lounger at the hotel, Cynthia sipped her mango and coconut drink. She was wearing a long salmon-pink tunic and wide white large trousers. Her eyes were hidden by mirrored sunglasses. She could see everything without being seen. Their group had arrived that evening. The journey had been exciting but exhausting. Flying for hours on end is bound to be tiring. But when they arrived, the city was so fascinating, the landscapes so magnificent, that all we wanted to do was recover. Enjoy the moment. This morning, the group of sisters was going to visit the city of Muscat. She was happy to have been able to save up for this little trip to Oman, which was organized every year by a Muslim association in her town. It was her first trip. She had never been out of her suburb, and even after she had her own small studio apartment, although independent, she had never dared to take such a trip. She felt too bold! Solena laughed gently at her. "A real baddie, wow!" As the dawn sun beat down on her face, she thought back to Samuel. How they had come so close to each other... and how they had parted. And the last look they'd exchanged the day before. Her former boss, who was well aware of her religious convictions, had taken great pleasure in putting them together in search of new pastries. They all had to work in pairs. Cynthia was not at all attracted to Samuel at first. And yet he was tall, athletic, handsome, and had intense and beautiful black-colored eyes. And a gorgeous smile. But the young woman found his beauty superficial and his personality superficial and hollow. And then, little by little, she had discovered a kind, funny and educated man. Unlike the other students, they both came from the same modest background, suburban communities with high unemployment. So they understood each other. They were motivated because it was an opportunity to help them to succeed in their life, to support their families, and to make a difference in a country and a society that had already labelled them because of their origin and religion. Together they had so many interesting discussions about it, while baking or when it was a break. "You can do this, Cynthia, and I'll be there to support you." "We will succeed both insha Allah." He supported her, congratulating her on her small successes. This constant support... This is what had created a breach in the heart of the young woman...

That evening complicity was replaced by a strong attraction for each other. Seriousness had given way to an atmosphere of joy and good mood and they started throwing water at each other in the middle of the kitchen and the utensils. And suddenly Samuel had stopped laughing. But still smiling, he looked at her with a look full of sweetness and desire. He approached her, gently wiping away the drops that trickled down Cynthia's lips and eyelids. She recalled the thrill that had swept over her at that moment. Closing her eyes under the warmth of his hand and fingers on her face. Torn between giving into the temptation, the desire that tormented her, and fleeing far away. Suddenly, Adhan was rung on her mobile. And she was suddenly brought back to reality. It was as if Allah wanted to protect her, at that moment when she felt herself slipping. She apologized, felt ashamed, and left Samuel. After changing and praying in one of the empty rooms in the factory, she left quickly. How she had invoked Allah that night, begging him to forgive her for letting herself go and to strengthen her faith. But above all, to make all her feelings for Samuel disappear! And the next day, she had distanced herself radically from him. Their co-project was well- advanced. Together, they had drawn up a menu of desserts and pastries for their forthcoming exam. She no longer had to stay late. She left the factory at the same time as the rest of the group. No longer would she arrive an hour or two before her other colleagues. In short, Cynthia avoided being alone with Samuel. She didn't answer his calls anymore either. She had given him her number just for work. And after her change of heart and that she distanced herself, the young man no longer called her. They only spoke when it was really necessary. But even during their brief exchanges, he looked her straight in the eye, still with that little smile in the corner of his lips, full of self- confidence, sure of the effect he still had on Cynthia. Finally, on the advice and encouragement of her friends, Cynthia ended up deleting for good his number because she herself felt the need to talk to him, to hear his warm voice on the other end of the line. She missed their conversations, his jokes, his laughter... It was on the evening of her resignation that she decided to start fresh. Then she did something crazy, at her own level. She signed up for a group trip to Oman. It was crazy because the cost of the trip was taking a serious toll on her savings. But she and Solena had decided that it was a treat they could afford because they needed a holiday so badly. "Money go but it will come back" Said Solena to resume... And also Cynthia wanted to get away from her worries and do some quiet thinking. She needeed to focus on what she really wanted. She didn't wait for a boyfriend or an eternal fiancé.

She wanted a husband, someone with whom to start a family, a man who would commit himself to her according to the Quran and the Sunna, and with whom she would evolve in this world with a view to Jannah. It was beautiful, isn't it? But she was convinced that nothing was impossible for Allah. You hear miraculous stories every day. So why not her? It was time she drew up a plan or rather her wedding plan. No, she wasn't going to let it get her down. Thinking back to the meeting she had made, and her bond with Samuel, she realized that what was wrong was that she didn't really know what criteria to use when looking for a husband. If she had known, she wouldn't have done so much, she wouldn't have been so impatient... And she wouldn't have been so vulnerable in front of Samuel, who was the opposite of her. Her project would therefore begin with a first objective: to forget him. it was obvious that none of his research was successful. How can you concentrate on the future if you're stuck in the past? With a new plan in mind, motivated and determined, she headed for the desk and took out a sheet of paper and a pen from the drawer. She was going to draw up a list of everything she was looking for in her future husband.

And this is the man she would marry insha'Allah! Does Allah not hear our invocations? But yesterday, just as she was putting down her luggage in Oman, her mobile rang:

It was Samuel.

Chapter 5

Guess Who's Here?

{The men, do they think we'll let them say: "We believe!" Without testing them? Yes, We tested those who lived before them. Allah is well acquainted with those who speak the truth, and He is well acquainted with those who lie.}

[**Surah 29-Verses 2-3**]

Jabir Ibn Abdullah reported: The Prophet (ﷺ) said: Whoever has faith in Allah the Last Day, let him not be secluded with an unrelated woman without her guardian lest Satan be the third of them.

[**Source: Musnad Aḥmad 14651**]

Cynthia was about to leave the hotel room with her friend when the telephone rang. "You can go downstairs, I'll join you insha'Allah," she said to her friend Solena. She picked up the phone, thinking about the buffet waiting for her downstairs. "Hello?? "Salam Cycy..." The young woman's heart leaped. When she heard Samuel's voice. She thought she was going to faint but feigned indifference. "Wa 'Alaikum salam" "Look, I know you don't want to talk to me but I won't be long. I think about you every day...And..." "We can discuss it when I get back from holiday," she cut him off. I haven't got time now, they're waiting for me." She pretended to be cold and indifferent, but in reality, her heart was racing in her chest. She was touched that he had taken the time to call her. It meant he cared about her. "Wait a minute, I've got a proposition for you." Skeptical and tense, Cynthia lay back on the bed. The voice of reason tried to clear her head. "Don't leave your base. He'll just lead you on, telling lies to your face. Girl! You don't hear me? The voice of reason shouted. But she could still scream... "Oh yeah... I'm hearing you...But not today." Thought Cynthia. "I'm listening." She said. Samuel continued: "I never thought I'd say this, but...I was thinking I'd love to wake up next to you for the rest of my life and hear your crazy laugh." "And I'm supposed to accept that?

What's so weird about my laugh?" Cynthia returned, pretending to be offended. She couldn't help to giggle and feel stupid. He too laughed. "Wait, I haven't finished. I want to marry you. I know you don't want to because I'm not practicing. But give me a chance. I've got something to give you, look at your phone." Cynthia heard her mobile vibrate. She had just received an MMS showing a gorgeous gold ring set with two medium-sized diamonds. She realized he was here. And how had he got her number? "Cycy...can I come over?" She was stunned. This crazy man had traveled all the way to Oman to give her a ring... and propose marriage! She smiled, unable to contain her joy at knowing he was here. Everything was jostling in her head and in her heart. She felt that, at last, she had been rewarded for her wait, for her determination to preserve herself. All had not been in vain hamdoulillah. "Okay, go ahead but it's just to put the ring back on. I don't want us to be alone and I don't want anyone to see us together. "Ah, when it comes to diamonds. ... " He said ironically. She hung up on him. In her room, she was smiling. Barely five minutes later, he was there. Outside her door, all clean and even more handsome than she remembered. He smelled of musk. She avoided looking at him because he made her uncomfortable. "Here." He handed her a small velvet box containing the famous ring. Cynthia couldn't help smiling. "BaarakAllahufeek, you've come a long way to give me this..."She said with emotion. He looked at her with a smile. "In fact, I'm also away on business. I've made a stopover. I'll be leaving again in a couple of hours." "Incha Allah", Cynthia added. She felt really happy. But the news made her feel slightly disappointed. She was glad that he was finally proving to her that he was ready to settle down with her. He was finally putting his words into action. He was there, despite all her efforts to avoid him, and that, for Cynthia, was proof that he really loved her. But at the same time, she was hesitant. "You came all this way...Just for me?"She thought it was a bit quick and didn't trust him completely. Samuel sensed this as he continued: "Anywhere to you, Cynthia. Do you remember? He said in a whisper.

He look at her intensely and smile. "You know how I feel about you. Give us a chance...I'll learn about religion with you, it doesn't have to be a barrier between us. Don't say anything for the moment, just think about it and give me your answer when you get back, okay?" "Ok, insha'Allah." She looked up at him and just then a sister crossed the corridor, glaring at her. Embarrassed, she said Salam and met the silence. Revolted by the sister's attitude, she wanted to shout at her that it was forbidden to ignore a salutation and was about to remind her of the correct behavior as a Muslim but... it wasn't really the right moment. "You're having a wonderful holiday, I see," Samuel said ironically. "You should go. I'll think about your proposal insha'Allah". While she was talking to him, a brother also appeared. He looked at them indifferently and continued on his way to the lift. "Maybe I should stay after all..." Samuel murmured when he saw the brother. "No, please go ahead. Thank you for this beautiful ring. I'm really happy but we'll talk about it when I get back, doing things properly insha'Allah". Samuel stared at her. But when she looked determined, he finally gave her a sign that he accepted her decision. "Ok, call me please" Cynthia closed the door. A wave of emotions washed over her. Samuel was above all a smooth talker. That was one of the things that had made her think at the time that he was superficial. His ability to be persuasive meant that he was able to get out of any difficult situation. He had a way of getting what he wanted...Which made her doubt his approach. OKAY, a marriage proposal, a ring...She was the kind of person who had an instinct about people... but didn't listen to herself, which often led her into tricky situations. Although she was enthusiastic about the idea of marrying him, her head told her it was a bad plan. Was he sincere with her? Leaning against the door, Cynthia looked at the ring Samuel had given her. It was exactly her size. She smiled. Her thoughts were suddenly interrupted by her mobile phone ringing. She'd just received a text message: "You like the ring?" The young woman barely had time to answer when she heard a knock on the door.

"I'll be leaving again soon...and I'd like to see your face first insha'Allah...I'm going to have a hard month at work." She opened the door, aware of the mistake she had made. He smiled at her. "Thanks, will you let me in?" Worried that they wouldn't be seen again, she complied and closed the door behind them. But she knew perfectly well that this was a mistake and a weakness on her part. "I'm glad you like the ring," said the young man. He was leaning against the bedroom door. "Who told you it was the case?" Cynthia replied. "You opened up to me and you're wearing the ring on your finger..." he added with a confident smile. "Anyway, now that you've seen my face... she replied ironically, you can go. The idea of her being alone with him in her room made her uncomfortable. "Not until I hear your witchy laugh." He said. At these words, Cynthia raised her hand to hit him in the chest, but he caught her hand quickly and drew the young woman to him. Against him, she felt every urge to resist him, to leave her. Desire was taking hold of her. And when he leaned in to kiss her, at first she was sorely tempted, then she turned her face, feeling his lips on her cheek. He didn't give up and Cynthia felt the hands of the man she loved running over her. Feverishly, he pulled her towards the bed. "The things I want to do to you...Cycy" He said in a breath. Just these few words gave back Cynthia all her lucidity; she stopped one of the Samuel's hands from slipping under her clothes and forced herself to push him away. "Stop it. She said in a whisper and moved away from him. "Stop! I don't want to! Not like this. If you really want to marry me, you'll have to wait." And she pulled herself out of his arms to sit up on the bed. "I'm sorry," said Samuel but Cynthia continued:"I don't feel respected here and because of you, I'm not going to stop thinking about what just happened." He laughed. "Was it that unpleasant?" "Oh, Is that really what you're interested in? We shouldn't even be having this discussion." Cynthia replied. "Given our feelings for one another, I don't see the problem" said Samuel. He was so peaceful, so confident in himself, it make her more upset. "That's the problem. This is not how I imagined my first time! With a man who's not my husband...and in a hotel room!" "Still a 4-star" replied the young man, teasing her. She realized then that he couldn't share her life. He was the opposite of everything she wanted, everything she believed in. In fact, he didn't care. When he came here, he already knew what he wanted. And if she'd given in, he wouldn't have done anything to stop her - he didn't really care whether she wanted to preserve herself or not. All he wanted was to possess her. She stood up to face him. "You don't understand. I have values. I believe in Allah, in Islam. And what just happened makes me sick! It makes me sick to want someone who will never share my point of view. Worse! Who drags me into everything that goes against my religion. If you don't share that, then we have nothing to do together." "So...Don't be sick! Accept that you find me irresistible. Don't get yourself into such a state, no one was killed. " Still lying there, he seemed detached and in no way upset by the young woman's state of mind... When Cynthia understood that, she arranged her clothes correctly and went 56

to open the bedroom door. She was furious with herself. And she felt stupid for having been about to give in. "I want you to leave". Samuel stood up. "Is this how you treat my commitment to you? Is my ring worthless?" As she arranged her hijab, Cynthia looked up at him. "That's not the point. If there really was a commitment, you would have held back. You don't respect me. For you, I'm just another challenge. If that's all you have to promise me, then it's more like a ticket to hell. "No thanks," she added. Samuel laughed furiously. "Hell? You created it for yourself. There's something strong between us. And you're rejecting it! You're hurting yourself and me too! We're human. We have desires. I don't see why I should be ashamed of the way I feel about you! Is it worth going to extremes? You'll never know what it's like to love if you keep holding back!" And now he was pretending to be a victim.

"Extremes? This is how you see religion? YOUR religion too? Because for me; it's not an extreme. These are the things I believe in and that are important to me. I don't see why you're chasing me. You knew why I didn't want to continue and why I left. In reality, it's impossible for us to be together. I don't want to give in in my desires...Because, I want to share intimacy with someone who understand me and who share my vision of life." She raised her hand to her chest, "My faith". Her eyes were brimming with tears as she continued, "You know that. I want to move on without regrets." Samuel got up and stood in front of Cynthia. "What are you afraid of? I came all the way here to propose, I love you sincerely. Why don't you trust me?"

"I'm not like all those girls you knew". Replied Cynthia, looking at him. "No. It's true! You're the most fake! And hypocrite. You think you can be with someone and have feelings for someone else? You can forget about me, us? No. And you know that. I don't forget you either." And the young man angrily headed for the door. Just as he was leaving, two sisters passed by, while chatting. Cynthia came out quickly to join him. "We have to go out separately. Too many people have seen us. I don't want people to get the wrong idea." Samuel looked at her and shook his head: "So what if it happened? Just lives a normal life!" Solena was also getting out of the lift. She walked towards them, her eyes wide. Shocked by Samuel's presence. Cynthia gestured to the young man to go ahead without her. "What's Samuel doing here?" whispered Solena. "Er..." Embarrassed, Cynthia didn't know what to say. With what had just happened, she understood the need not to travel alone. If she had been accompanied by a mahram, none of this would have happened. And he would never dare to show up. Everything had happened so quickly.

Samuel had taken advantage of this moment when he knew she would be vulnerable and alone. Perhaps he hadn't been looking for what had just happened, but the result was the same "You didn't tell me Samuel was coming. What's he doing here?" Cynthia felt herself tense up. Before things got out of hand, she preferred to tell the truth. "I'll explain everything tonight, I promise, insha'Allah. It's very complicated." Later in the restaurant, she deliberately chose to sit with some sisters. It was crowded. The waiters were busy. There was also a large buffet where people were grouped together to serve themselves one after the other. The large windows gave a stunning view of the beach and the sea, which was calm that afternoon. Cynthia tried to take part in the conversations as naturally as possible. Solena was giving her eloquent looks but refrained from bombarding her with questions... A few tables away, Samuel was eating while supporting her with his gaze. "Why don't you eat with your husband?" The sister, who had met them in the corridor the first time and had not responded to her Salam, was staring at her. Cynthia got up to join her 'husband' so that she wouldn't end up having to justify herself to her. When she arrived, Samuel was getting up to leave. "I'm going...know that I love you, no matter what you think of me. I'm off again. I hope by then you'll have thought about us both" Without the slightest regard for the people around them, he planted himself in front of her and stared at her. He felt like caressing her face but refrained from doing so because Cynthia looked so mortified. He left without looking back. "The group taking a tour of the city of Muscat, please join me at the reception!" The voice snapped Cynthia out of her thoughts. The brother who had passed earlier in the corridor was standing in the middle of the restaurant.

Their eyes met.

Chapter 6

What If It Was Him?

"It may be that you hate something when it is good for you. And it may be that you love something, while it is harmful to you. It is Allah Who knows, while you know not" [**Surah Al Baqarah, verse 216**].

Cynthia had not enjoyed of her visit to Muscat. Her mind was too preoccupied with her "accident" with Samuel because even though she had a strong attraction for the young man, she had a feeling of guilt for letting herself be seduced. She knew deep down that she had made the best decision. The Prophet (ﷺ) said : « Verily you will never leave anything for the sake of Allah Almighty but that Allah will replace it with something better for you ». She had to hold on on it in spite of her feelings for Samuel. In spite of her promise to marry her.

The scenery was magnificent. The bustling city, the smiling faces of the Omani people, the musk on the stalls, the abayas, the colorful fabrics, and the gold jewelry in the shops, distracted her but couldn't stop her mind from wandering and lifting her spirits. She walked alongside the sisters, laughing at conversations, but her heart wasn't in it. Solena noticed this and took her aside. "You didn't buy any souvenirs...even though we told Miriam we'd bring her something." Cynthia looked at her and finally told her everything. She knew she could trust Solena... and count on her ability to cheer her up. She was a naturally cheerful girl, her smile warmed your heart and she had a lot of wisdom in her. She was the first to marry. When she was 19, she met a young man with whom she became a couple. She got pregnant and they ended up getting married. Unfortunately, he was an abusive man and the girls witnessed Solena's transformation.

She had withdrawn into herself and cared only about her children. And although she kept in touch with her friends, she no longer saw them. Her husband exerted such an influence that the young woman gradually cut herself off from the outside world. It was when she sensed the danger to her children and understood that they were going to grow up in a climate of violence, that she summoned up all her courage and decided to leave. It was Miriam who picked her up by car. Her own parents knew nothing about it. The young woman had never dared confide in them that their ideal son-in-law was in fact a manipulative and violent man. She underwent therapy and converted to Islam. With the support of her family and friends, Solena was now a strong woman mentally and spiritually. And for Miriam and Cynthia, she was now more than a friend, she was also their fi Allah sister. For this holiday, she had left her children with her mother and father. And she intended to enjoy her stay. It wasn't easy for her to look after children alone and at the same time find time for herself. Cynthia decided to confide in her and told her everything. "Okay, I understand. But you know what? Everybody makes mistakes. You have feelings for him and I'm sure he knew he wouldn't have to do much to make you give in. But, AlHamdulillah, you didn't take the plunge. Now you really know who you're dealing with... and that's all that matters. "But that's just it! What if, on the contrary, he was the right one? What if he changed after we got married? He did come all the way here with a ring!" Solena pretended to bang her head against a wall. "Aah no! You're not going to tell me you're one of those girls who gets taken in by nice words and a ring? Honestly, if he was really the one, he'd have shown a minimum of restraint, don't you think? It wasn't you who wrote on your famous list: "Pious and *practicing* brother? Is leading you into fornication something a pious and practicing brother would have you do?"

Cynthia said no. In fact, it was the criteria, the basis, that she had written down first. « Well, stay out of trouble, then.

Remember when Henry gave me a hard time and then came back to me with a packet of candies? » Cynthia remembered that day very well indeed. Henry, the ex-husband from before Solena's conversion to Islam. One day, he had humiliated her in a shop, after the young woman had refused to walk beside him because he spoke badly to her. He grabbed her violently by the back of the neck and spoke badly to her in front of everyone. People didn't react until he shook her, still grabbing her by the back of the neck. " Two men and a woman had come to separate them. Solena had left quickly, going to Miriam's house to spend the night. Cynthia joined them. That evening, Henry came over with a packet of Solena's favorite Haribo to apologize. As if nothing had happened. He told her he was sorry, but that it was her fault that he'd snapped. Solena stood in front of him, the marks of her fingers still visible on his neck, her eyes red with tears. The scene had been so surreal that, 4 years later, the girls still remembered it as if it had happened yesterday. But even after that, Solena was back with him. The very next day. She had become pregnant again, and the girls had resigned themselves to seeing their friend still in denial. At the time, they would never have believed her capable of leaving. But by the grace of Allah, she finally did it. The kind of memory that makes you say it's better to laugh than to cry. "What I want to tell you, 'Thia, is that he's not going to change overnight. If he's already showing you he can't be trusted and clearly doesn't respect your boundaries when you're not married, what's it going to be like when you will be? Come here. And Solena put her arm around her friend's shoulders. « You have to trust Allah's plan because He has always better plan for us. » She said while hugging her friend. « And you mean too much to me to let you throw your life away. We'll find you a *Franco* and you'll finally leave that stupid book behind, insha'Allah." "Imagine if I said that about your favorite film ?" said Cynthia, pretending to be offended. Solena removed her arm and looked at her, "Are you really going to compare this 7-time award- winning Masterpiece, based on a book that changed people's lives...to this shit show?" Cynthia interrupted her by putting her hand over her mouth. They both laughed. The discussion continued as they talked about their marriage prospects and were soon joined in their conversation by other single girls in the group. It was a very rich exchange. There was so much to say on the subject! Surprisingly, although their religion encouraged them to marry, it was a project that was becoming almost difficult to achieve. Cynthia was feeling relaxed at last, she hadn't been wrong. Her friend had a real gift for making her forget her worries. Later, back at the hotel, the girls split up and went to their own rooms. Some of them shared a double room. She and Solena had taken the same room. They chatted for a while, raving about everything they'd seen on their outing, and then Solena locked herself in the bathroom for a moment to wash up. She soon came out again. She wanted to Facetime with her children. She missed them too much. When it was her turn, Cynthia took a long, hot shower, but it wasn't enough to relax her. She remembered Samuel's lips, his passionate yet gentle caresses... Once she had dried off, she looked at herself in the mirror. He had called her a hypocrite. It was probably true. She had welcomed him into her room, expecting what might happen. And she knew deep down that she wasn't going to marry him. She couldn't, her heart was pulling her towards him but her head was telling her to stay as far away as possible. He was a manipulator. He knew exactly how to make her let her guard down. He knew how important marriage was to Cynthia. If she had let herself go, he would only have encouraged her, because what he liked most was to see her resist. But then, what would have happened? Would he have married her? She remembered clearly one day when she had overheard him talking to a colleague about the women he had already been with. The game, the power, that was played between them, and he ranked them from the easiest to the most difficult... and apparently, according to him, there hadn't been many in the last category. So, before their boss got them together, she talked to him as little as possible and kept some distance. But that was before she got to know him, before the long discussions and moments of complicity. She wondered whether he was sincere, or whether he just wanted to make a new Trophy of her... There was a world separating them and none of them were willing to take the risk. But she had accepted that he would come over and give her the ring, she had wanted to believe it. And she understood Samuel's anger, she had given him a semblance of hope. But she also felt that she had made the best decision. As her big sister used to say by appropriating a famous George Washington sentence: "It's better to be alone than in bad company". She was mortified to be experiencing so many contradictory feelings. The desire, the love, the urge to join Samuel, to give in temptation, and her aspiration to hold back and be a better believer by worshipping her Creator in obedience. His heart and head were in whirling. "Subhanallah how hard is it!" She prayed and invoked Allah as much as she could. With all her heart. Then she went to bed. Her friend was already asleep. After long minutes of cogitating, and sleep not coming, Cynthia got up, did a nawafil prayer, recited her invocations, and then read a page of the Quran. She came across this verse in the surat al- Ma`idah The Table: *"But whoever repents after their wrongdoing and mends their ways, Allah will surely turn to them in forgiveness. Indeed, Allah is All- Forgiving, Most Merciful. As for him who repents after having done wrong, and makes amends, Allah will accept his repentance."* This calmed her down. Her aim was to finish reading the whole thing before the end of the summer holidays.

Then she took out her tablet to read "Love with the Wind" on Wattpad: "I'd never abandon you, I'd rather go back to prison than leave you to that loser" Astafara batted her long eyelashes as she looked at Antonio. "We'll be together forever insha Allah, marry me! He jumped on his motorbike and roared off". "Fly my love, Fly". Thought Astafara. "Worst book I've ever read, I can't believe they're going to adapt it for Netflix..." she heard herself think before drifting off to sleep. In the night, her phone vibrated. It was Samuel.

Chapter 7

Alone and Abandonned

"Lord, I am in great need of any grace that You will kindly grant me".
[Mûsa 'alayhi salam, surat 28 Al Qasas, verse 24]

The next day, the whole group gathered in the hotel entrance. Some of the girls came with their families. "We're leaving for the Omani dunes in 20 minutes insha'Allah. Don't forget to take the essentials, like a bottle of water, hat or cap...the list is posted over there at the end of the corridor". Their guide was the brother she had met yesterday, Cynthia noticed. He was tall and good looking. Clean and fresh, you could tell he was athletic and took good care of himself. She didn't dislike him, but Cynthia thought he seemed overconfident. She even thought he looked a little mean...or cold. But without knowing why she felt intrigued by him. "He's just taking himself too seriously," she thought. He moved towards her, without looking directly at her. "Sister, I'd advise you to change your shoes. We're going hiking, not shopping." Cynthia raised her eyebrows of stupefaction. She looked down at her new white Puma shoes, the satin ribbons served as laces. He had spoken normally without raising his voice, but she felt insulted. "What a way to talk to customers! She thought. "I don't have any hiking boots." She said as she felt upset by his comment. When she looked at him he seemed amused and but his eyes were full of kindness. But he didn't let her poor excuse put him off. "Perhaps you could check with some of the other sisters or perhaps see if your husband can't bring you some?" Cynthia's heart clenched. "My husband?" She pulled herself together as she remembered Samuel. "Aaah yes my husband...we've...er we've separated...permanently. He's not coming back." Then she added: "Never." The brother looked surprised. His eyes were full of questions. But he said nothing. Embarrassed for her, he just said "I'm sorry". Then there was a brief silence that seemed to Cynthia like a long moment of eternity. After all those lies, she was

43

already imagining Divine punishment. The young man interrupted her thoughts. "May Allah make it easy for you. I'll see with my sister if she can't lend you the right shoes insha Allah." And it was Cynthia's turn to be surprised: the sister in question was none other than the one she'd met in the hallway and who'd almost ordered her to go and sit with Samuel... Once she'd changed her shoes, she thanked the girl who ignored her and went back with a group of women. "Great family." Later, in the 4x4 as they set off across the Omani dunes, Cynthia, alongside Solena, admired the landscape with rapture. The sun was so strong that it was difficult for them to admire all this beauty without sunglasses. The heat was heavy but bearable. The dunes were magnificent and seemed to stretch on forever. Early in the morning, when she had woken up for prayers, she had seen that Samuel had sent her a message apologising for his behaviour. And how much he cared for her. He wanted her to give him another chance. And he suggested that they meet with a view to marriage. During this she could ask him all the questions she wanted. "We've never done that before". Indeed, the young woman realised that she had never thought of making properly a marriage meeting with Samuel. In the end, she agreed. After all, it would allow her to make the right decision about them. Perhaps, after all, he was sincere... When they arrived, the people in charge of the charity, the brother and his colleague had set up camp. The whole group had travelled in 4x4s. Two more cars arrived. The afternoon was full of discovery and adventure. Oman was truly a splendid country. Then it was off to the tents to eat and pray. While the organisers were engaged in preparing for departure, Cynthia took the opportunity to walk around and admire the landscape. Sometimes she stopped to take a selfie. On the way back... and to add to her private Instagram page. She had 20 followers. Family, classmates and friends. She was not really into social media but who knows why, she still created an insta and linkedin page for work. She thought briefly of her younger sister who had a TikTok account with 1,300 followers. She posted mostly "emo-depressing-rebellious- misunderstood-by-adults" stuff. Cynthia let out a chuckle as she thought: "She'll probably be interested in that picture of the desert for some existential posts...". From time to time, she would turn around to see if the others were still there. Solena was in the middle of a discussion with a group of sisters, holding a small child who seemed to be crying uncontrollably. No one had noticed that she was far away. "I've got to clean my sunglasses". As she was going through the pockets of her backbag, she accidentally dropped the ring. But she didn't realise it and walked away to find a good angle for her selfie and take better photos of the landscape. A little later, as she turned back towards the group, she noticed that her ring was no longer in the bag. Then she retraced her steps, desperately looking for the ring Samuel had given her. She didn't know how much it had cost, but the jewellery in question looked expensive. And given the uncertain outcome of their relationship, it didn't occur to her to keep anything from him. She had to give him back his ring ASAP insha Allah. She began to search in the warm sand, groping here and there, even walking on all fours, looking carefully at the sand and plunging her hand into it.

The further she went, the more indistinct the voices became. It was only when the sun began to fade that she realised that the time had passed. Panicking, she climbed back up the dune and returned to the campsite, but no one was there. It was then that she realised she had strayed too far. "But how could they forget me?" The cold had replaced the heat. "I'm going to die alone and abandoned because of a stupid ring from a man I'm not even going to marry." "Aaaaah! Shit!" Her cry of rage echoed in the silence of the desert. "Astargfirullah, al hamdulillah", she said suddenly. "I mustn't panic or I'll go mad. She remembered the verse: *Surely we belong to Allah and to Him we shall return.*" When she'll go back to France, she wouldn't hesitate to leave a salty review on Google! She looked in her bag for her smartphone, desperately. The battery was low. But the last remaining bar convinced her to call the hotel. When the operator picked up, the phone went dead. She saw only the words "Samsung" disappear from the screen against a black background, and then the mobile suddenly switched off. "Noooo stupid phone!!!" But what's the point of technology if you're just going to leave people to die in the middle of the desert? Like WHAT'S THE POINT? This is divine punishment, she thought. Yes, it was.

For having almost succumbed to Samuel. What if this was the end for her? She was about to make out with Samuel. Then she lied. That was all she deserved. She sat down on the sand. Despite the cold, it was still warm. She drew her legs together against her chin. "O Allah, forgive me and let me go home. I won't go near Samuel or anyone else until the wedding". She stood up determined. "I've got to go home". She walked but she didn't know where to go. No phone, no compass. Only hope guided her. She also made the invocation that she used to make almost every time she was tested: "O Lord, there is nothing easy but what you have made easy and, by your will, trouble becomes easy".

Her feet, in her too-large shoes, sank into the sand with every step she took. Her stomach was starting to rumble because she was hungry. "If I'd known I was going to be stuck here, I'd have eaten that sandwich... She didn't have a drop of water left, but she didn't feel dehydrated yet. She thought back to those cartoons where the character is lost in the desert and starts delirious and seeing oases... Let's hope it doesn't come to that, insha'Allah". She could feel the panic starting to get there. Perhaps an hour or two had passed. In fact, how could she know? She had lost track of time and managed to locate in time thanks to the last prayer she did before. It wouldn't be long before nightfall. Now she was really panicking. Anything could happen to her. She recited her protective surah. The best thing was not to give in to fear and rely on Allah. Everything happens for a reason. Cynthia paused, searching through her bag for something to eat or drink. Suddenly, she heard a whirring noise. "I hope they're not psychopaths...or desert pirates." She'd vaguely heard about it one day, in a documentary on YouTube. She thought she just had her mini antiperspirant. "I'm not sure it can replace a pepper spray". Cynthia was still rummaging through her bag, looking for something to defend herself, when she saw the cause of the noise. She raised her arms and waved. It must have been tourists. A 4x4 drove towards her and soon stopped in front of her. She felt suddenly relieved. The man bent his head out of the window: "Looks like you got lost?" She recognised the guide behind the steering wheel.

Chapter 8

Saved! And A nice Boy OMG

{And tell the believing women to lower their gaze, to keep their chastity, and not to show their finery except as it appears, and that they should draw their veils over their breasts; And that they show their finery only to their husbands, or to their fathers, or to their husbands' fathers, or to their sons, or to their husbands' sons, or to their sisters' sons, or to Muslim women, or to the slaves they own, or to impotent male servants, or to impubescent boys who know nothing of the hidden parts of women. And let them not strike with their feet so that it may be known what they hide in their finery.

And repent all of you before Allah, O believers, so that you may reap success.}

[Surah 24, verse 31]

Exhausted by her walk through the desert, with the beginnings of a headache from the sun beating down on her head, Cynthia looked at the brother who was watching her with a slightly worried expression. "Come on, get in the car. I'll take you back insha'Allah." He was accompanied by his sister. She greeted her again. This time, the woman replied. In the car, she internally thanked Allah for helping her. How scared she had been! To die alone and abandoned, or being attacked by a beast or desert pirates... yes, her imagination had never bubbled so much. She felt achy and her feet hurt. She rested her head against the backrest. The open window let the warm wind come in and sweep across her face. She felt nauseous. Inside the car, the silence was heavy. She remembered that the guide had saved her: "Thank you". The young man didn't reply. Concentrating on the road, he replied without looking at her. "You put yourself in danger. It's a good thing we noticed you were missing, otherwise, you'd probably have died here. You're completely unconscious!" added the young man. "I know, thank you," she thought but said nothing. She took his remarks as a slap in the face.

But she remembered that it was the guide's role to ensure the safety of the group. "I don't agree with you" The pain twisted his temples. "You should have checked that everyone was present. I think it's a bit rich to blame me. You should be apologizing for putting me in danger!

Cynthia felt that she had touched a sensitive point because the brother said nothing in return. She was sorry that her friend Solena hadn't noticed her absence, she was sorry that she had wandered away from the camp... She felt a bit foolish.

"I'm sorry. And I apologize. You're right, I'm sorry. I almost lost my job. Luckily, my uncle is the hotel manager. That helps. But to lose someone in the middle of an excursion... It's very bad publicity." Hiding behind his aviator sunglasses, she saw him smiling in the rear-view mirror. He seemed obviously enjoy his joke. Cynthia shook her head, feeling all the anger of having been abandoned come flooding back. "I think you would have deserved it, it's really incompetence, I can press charges you know?..I...feel...bad, I'm going to puke." Her heart was pounding. And with the 4x4 shaking her in all directions, it was only getting worse. Her stomach felt like it was going to come up through her throat. The guide brought the car to a sudden halt. The dunes surrounded them. Cynthia got out. At times like this, nothing matters. She threw up beside the car. She saw the sister, who had stayed in the car, grimace with disgust. Honestly, she couldn't have cared less and she felt a sense of satisfaction as she remembered that she had swapped her new Puma shoes for a pair of hiking boots... which didn't belong to her... and whose owner was watching her throw up the depths of her womb. By the time she'd finished, she was feeling a little bit better. "Are you all right? Come on, have some water." The young man, who had pulled his glasses up over his head, was handing her a bottle of mineral water. Her throat was on fire, she couldn't hesitate. Realizing that she'd emptied most of it, she wanted to give it back to him... automatically. "It's okay...you can keep it, it's a gift. He said ironically Cynthia wanted to smile, but she didn't even have the strength. She was sweating and her headache hadn't been alleviated completely by the vomiting.

She got back into the car, which started straight away. The sister turned to her: "Close the window so you don't catch a cold, the temperature has dropped quite a bit". "Yes... Later. Right now I need some air. » « What's your name?"Asked the brother. "Cynthia." "Okay Cynthia, I'm Liam and this is my sister Kassandra. We have a nurse on site who can examine you insha'Allah." She wasn't in the mood for small talk. "Okay" But the brother continued: "I didn't mean to be harsh earlier, but you're right, I bear a greater share of the responsibility for what happened to you. If I hurt you, apologize again. We'll make sure you're reimbursed for the cost of the trip." For the first time, she detected an ounce of gentleness in his gaze. Crossing his gaze in the rear- view mirror, she noticed that he had beautiful hazel eyes, flecked with green. She looked away. His eyes were truly hypnotic. "No, you were right too, I should have been careful. I could have died just because I wanted to find the right angle for my selfies... » They both laughed briefly and there was silence again. But the climate had changed. The ice had been broken. "You're not going to press charges then?" Kassandra asked in a slightly haughty tone. Cynthia looked at her and smiled. "No, you practically saved me Alhamdulillah". The whole hotel seemed to be asleep when they arrived. The three of them walked to the reception desk. There Liam spoke to the receptionist. He said Salams to Kassandra and he and Cynthia went their separate ways. Five minutes later, an elderly veiled woman took Cynthia into a small room that served as an infirmary. She gave her some paracetamol, checked her eyes, and let her go. She advised her to drink plenty of water beforehand. When Cynthia went outside, Liam was waiting for her.

"The restaurant is still open so you can eat" he said. « No need to say more ! I'm soo hungry, salaaam ! » Cynthia left quickly, under the amuzed gaze of the young man. She was starving. Later, when the young woman walked through the door of her room, she was greeted by Solena and the other sisters. "We've been waiting for you. We're so sorry we forgot about you!

The girls hugged her. "Next time, we'll hook you up to a GPS." Solena in particular was feeling really guilty. "I was with a family, helping out with the kids. I thought you were hanging out with the others." Cynthia told her about what's happened in the desert and the stat the guide her found her. Later, when everyone had left, she went back down to meet the nurse as she still have some headhache. The nurse insisted saying to Cynthia that she needed to rest and hydrate. After a good shower, she was happy to be back in bed with fresh sheets. She fell asleep completely exhausted. The good thing was that at least she hadn't thought about Samuel all day. The next day, the young woman enjoyed to stay at the hotel. After her misadventure the day before, she had seen enough of the desert anyway. She spent the day sleeping and eating (the hotel's buffet dishes were so tasty! especially the biryani). She noticed that the Omanis had a lot in common with the Indians and Pakistanis when it came to food. The young woman was delighted to read by the huge heavenly pool. In the evening, she had met with her friends, who had just returned from their excursion to the dunes. "You missed everything! Solena told her, and she went on to tell her all about their outing. "The best of the week and we hadn't lost anyone". She added with a big ironic smile. Later, Cynthia went back down to the poolside, settling into her official lounge chair. A book in her hand, and a light shawl covering her shoulders. She was wearing a beige hijab and a long white abaya buttoned at the front and matched with white ballet flats shoes. There was nobody around the pool. Through the windows of the hotel restaurant, one or two waiters could still be seen bustling about. Absorbed in her reading, she didn't see the water move. Suddenly she saw Liam emerged from the turquoise water, dressed only in a pair of mid-length swimming shorts. She was taken aback by the sight of his firm, toned body, the muscles of which stood out even more after the effort. She felt her mouth open in amazement.

And she hastened to lower her gaze. Salam Aleykum," he said, grabbing a t-shirt and towel from the back of a chair. He looked at her briefly , " Are you feeling better?" "Wa..aleykoum salam, yes, yes!" Said the young woman with exaggerated enthusiasm and embarrassment at the same time... "I'm much better, thanks! I slept well!" she exclaimed as the brother was already walking away. She replayed the scene: "Did I say that I slept well? Bravo! I behaved like a pick-me girl...He didn't even ask me if I'd slept well, why did I say that? » Whenever she came face to face with a man who intimidated her, She always said something weird. She wanted to go back to her book but had some difficulty getting back into it. "He is actually quite nice and really...good looking man," she said with a small smile to herself. "I think the same thing. Cynthia turned her head and saw an elderly lady, who was wearing a straw hat and dark glasses. The woman was seated two chairs away. "If I were you, I wouldn't have wasted time." She winked at her with a big smile and went back to reading her magazine.

That evening, Cynthia sat down in front of the small desk in her bedroom and took out a sheet of paper from her notebook on which she had written down all the characteristics, qualities, etc. that she wanted to find in her future husband. It did not commit to anything, but for Liam, she had already ticked off 6 things that she would like to see in her future husband insha Allah... He was polite, caring, nice, charming...and able to question himself and apologize if needed.

With a smile, she closed the notebook. She took out her Fiqh lessons and studied for 20 minutes. Then she turned off the light and went to bed, smiling.

Chapter 9

We are Stunned By Him masha Allah, and Oh jealousy

"They raised their heads, saw his incredible beauty, and forgetting that they had knives in their hands, literally in a trance in front of this man, accidentally cut themselves. Then they described Joseph ('alayhi salam) as a noble angel.

[**Story of the Prophet Yusuf 'alayhi salam**]

Without knowing why, Cynthia got up that morning in a good mood. For the trip, she wore an off- white tunic and a camel- colored sarouel to match her hijab. In addition to her mobile phone, she packed a digital camera, lip balm, a towel, her burkini, monoi, some food, and a bottle of water. Today, their group was heading for the Bani Wadi Khaled, to enjoy the natural pools with their turquoise waters. All the sisters in the group were looking forward to going for a swim. It was a place well-known for its beauty and as a must-see tourist spot in Oman. The journey was made in 4x4, crossing the dunes. The splendid land never ceased to amaze them. Once there, everyone took their place. Cynthia saw some of her sisters join their husbands and children. She stayed with her group of sisters on the rocks and she stayed not far from the basins, the waters of which were clear and luminous. The afternoon was spent in good ambiance and relaxation. The children bathed under the close supervision of their parents. The women were able to swim in secluded spots, out of sight, or in the company of their husbands for those who were married. Cynthia took photos of the turquoise water and didn't forget to take selfies for her family and friends. She felt happy and fulfilled, there in this wonderful secluded landscape far from everything. No worries, no one judging you, everything was fine. And she was delighted to enjoy it. She pulled her glasses up over her hijab. The sun was still beating down, so she put her camera away and climbed a small rock to sit down and relax. Sitting high up, she could see the whole landscape and her group. Solena was a little way off with two other sisters. They were wearing burkinis over which they had donned long T-shirts. They took turns throwing water at each other and laughing as they tried to dodge water jets. Cynthia shared their enthusiasm even from a distance. In France, the country of their birth, they wouldn't be able to let off so much steam in a public place. They'd have to rent small private villas where a Muslim woman was free to swim in a bikini or a swimming clothes... But public places and swimming pools were no longer accessible to them.

For a while, some gym opened their pools in a clandestine way, and you had to register in advance on the list, by telephone...And then the ban was extended to the beaches. You were no longer allowed to wear a veil or even a burkini. The authorities didn't hesitate to kick you off the beach... She swept these negative things from her head. It was time to take pleasure in the freedom offered by this country and its breathtaking scenery. As for the rest, there was still a good week to go before returning home. She would be joining the girls a little later, insha'Allah. On the other side, she recognized Liam swimming with his colleague, leaping into the void to dive into the transparent turquoise water. He seemed to be enjoying himself like a child. In fact, she saw him swim to the shore where two children jumped on him, clinging to his strong arms. She felt that she was attracted by the young man and was not able to move her eyes from him.

Liam pulled the children clinging to his arms back into the water, making them laugh. "He'd probably be a good father," thought the young woman. She noticed that he had a scar just above his knee. "I've got really good eyesight...that's funny, I didn't see that yesterday...Oh, man...but what am I doing? Cynthia remembered the verse from the Surah An- Nur, which made perfect sense. *"Tell the believing men to lower their eyes (and do not look lustfully) and guard their private parts. That is purer (and better) for them. And Allah is well aware of what they do"* Astaghfirullah, I've got to stop now. I didn't come here for that! »

"Nice view, isn't it?" Cynthia gasped at the haughty voice and immediately snapped out of her thoughts, clumsily putting her sunglasses back on her nose, she looked up, ashamed to have been caught in the act. "I..I..oh..yes, nice view." Her interlocutor was none other than Liam's sister. Tall and beautiful in her pale pink abaya. She was wearing Dior glasses. Since the accident in the desert, Cynthia had realized that Kassandra was part of the organizing group, but she didn't seem very involved. "Don't bother. You were looking at my brother. Aren't you supposed to be married?" Shocked by his lack of politeness, Cynthia imagined, as in the cartoons, jumping into the water and swimming away from this viper. Instead, she stayed stuck to her rock. What was she supposed to say? "The brother you saw in my room was just my colleague, we aren't married?". Lying... how she hated it... She was terribly angry about it and knew that sooner or later it would come back to bite her... but everyone had seen them and she didn't want anyone to give her a reputation. "It's none of your business". And it was true. "That's a funny answer?" This girl is really shameless, Subhanallah!

« I'm not used to talking about my private life...especially to strangers..." She insisted on this last point as she looked at the young woman. hoping she loses interest in her and leaves. But she didn't. "It's funny because last time, you and the brother seemed to be pretty close. But hey, kheir incha Allah. What's your name again? "This is Cynt... But Kassandra cut her off abruptly. "Whatever. I'm going." And the young woman left, beautiful and venomous, leaving Cynthia drained of energy and shocked. "I hope she's not going to spread her venom about me... She thought. She hated this kind of person who not only didn't interfere in their own business but also never missed an opportunity to cause some trouble or gossip. On the way home, Cynthia thought about the moment that had somewhat ruined her afternoon. Later, she joined her friend Solena in the bedroom of two other girls. They had organized a little pajama party. There was a lot of chatting and snacking. The 2 owners of the room had beauty masks on their faces, a kind of thick green clay paste, and one of them was wearing a shower cap. "This brother is so handsome Masha Allah, he's driving me crazyyy". All the girls burst out laughing. One of them continued: "He's single, and what's more, I don't understand how that can happen but don't worry, he's my future husband insha'Allah. "You're dreaming, he's mine insha Allah!" And the girls burst out laughing again.

"I've noticed that every night he goes swimming..." It was the one in the bathing cap who had just spoken. "Are you seriously going to spy on him?" said her friend. "Not at all! May Allah protect me. I'm not that desperate". "In this situation, I don't mind being desperate" replied one of the girls in a tone of confidence. The others laughed. "How do you know that then?" Katy, the girl in the bathing cap, shrugged her shoulders. "My room overlooks the hotel swimming pool," she says as if it were obvious. Despite herself, Cynthia felt a pinch of jealousy in her heart. Apparently, quite a few sisters liked Liam...who were single...and some of them were much prettier than she was. "Anyway, I don't care. I didn't come here to get married but to have fun and relax..." She said to reassure herself. "Cynthia, did you spend a bit of time with him last time?" the young woman snapped out of her thoughts when she heard her name. "He just picked me up and dropped me off at the hotel, nothing to worry about or to tell...and there was her sister." The girls looked at her as if she had secrets to deliver. "Girls, I'm sorry, but apart from the fact that he's gorgeous, polite, and nice, I'm not going to tell you anything more," she laughed. "And you don't like him?" asked Solena with a mischievous look. "Not really. And I'm not ready for another disappointment anyway." In truth, she was tired of her marital adventures, which had seriously damaged her confidence. Later, she went back to her room to get her tablet and some change for a drink at the restaurant. The girls had thought about eating, but as far as drinks were concerned, there were only fizzy drinks, and the only bottle of water was already finished. In the restaurant, waiting

56

for her non-alcoholic fruit cocktail to be served, she read her book avidly. "How to behave with others according to the Sunnah? Sounds interesting." Cynthia looked up to see Liam sitting at the bar next to her. He was probably on his way to the prayer room as he was wearing a Qamis. His beard, neither too long nor too short, was carefully groomed. As well as his wonderful musky scent, he gave off an impression of strength and virility. He smiled, which only added to his charm. "Sorry to bother you. I have something to give to you." He placed a small sparkling object on the table. It was the ring Samuel had given her. He was about to leave, but Cynthia questioned him: "Where did you find it?" "Yesterday, as you mentioned a ring, I searched where we had set up camp. I have a metal detector, which is very useful when our tourists re-enact the hadith of 'Aïsha (radhi 'ala anha)". At first, Cynthia didn't understand the allusion and then she remembered the hadith which recounted the day when the wife of the Prophet (ﷺ) had lost her necklace in the desert . The people thought that she had gone back with them, but they had forgotten about her. "Ah yes, that's funny." She said, taking a sip of her cocktail. "I've got to laugh or he'll think I've got no sense of humor" Cynthia laughed a forced laugh, but as she'd just had a drink, she swallowed hard and had an uncontrollable coughing fit, so much so that the brother pretended to want to pat her on the back but the young woman signaled that she was fine. She finally stopped coughing. "Are you okay?" She placed her glass on the table. The people around them looked at her with concern...or curiosity. Sweating, her eyes slightly red from tears, she tried to give herself some composure despite the shame. What doesn't kill, makes you stronger, isn't that what they say? "Who would have thought that laughing and drinking are dangerous for your health? eh eh " Oh God, why am I so embarrassing?" The brother smiled at her, more concerned for her than mocking her. "Sit down in the armchair. I'll get you a glass of water". Cynthia sat back, replaying the scene in her mind. "An epic moment to write down in the book of my life" Nah what a shame! The brother returned with the glass of water, which he placed in front of her.

"It's time for salat. I must go. Salam aleykum" And he left, "Wa 'aleykum salam". Cynthia watched him go and she stood up.

She could feel her heart racing.

Chapter 10

Soulmate

(Aisha (radhi 'ala anha) reported that the Prophet (ﷺ) said: "Souls are like conscripted soldiers: Those who are like qualities are inclined to each other, but those who have dissimilar qualities, differ." **[Saheeh Al- Bukharî]**

The next day, Cynthia was at the cocktail bar. It was a beautiful place. And not an ounce of alcohol. She appreciated the fact that the hotel preserved its Islamic values despite the non- Muslim and international residents. She was enjoying her drink with Solena, who was telling her all about her difficulties with the latest marriage app, 'Myhalallove'. "Didn't we say we were ditching the apps?" Solena sat up straight in her chair. She was wearing large sunglasses that completely hid her eyes. "I know you're not convinced, but Myhalallove has some good reviews. You just have to sort out profiles. And honestly, I can't stand being single anymore, I'm going to lose my mind!" And with a dramatic air, she added in a whisper, "A woman has desires, my dear". Cynthia laughed. Then she saw Liam and his sister walking in the distance, chatting away. Her sister approached the girls, while Liam continued on his way. Not without looking quickly at Cynthia. " I felt electricity there!" "Cynthia slapped Solena thigh, "Don't embarrass me!" "Salam aleykum, are you available?" Kassandra, looking only at Cynthia. Solena, shocked at being ignored, lowered her glasses to look at the young woman. "Salam aleykum, I'm Solena, her friend". Kassandra looked at her indifferently.

"Wa aleykum salam, Cynthia's friend". Solena rolled her eyes and pushed up her glasses. "I'm available, yes" replied Cynthia, not really appreciating Kassandra's attitude. She finished her sentence by looking at Solena. Solena stood up but Cynthia motioned for her to sit back down. "That's fine, don't worry." Then by speaking to Kassandra "Let's sit over there". She showed her a place with some armchairs. "I'll be right back," she said, addressing Solena. Settling into the armchairs in the small lounge,Cynthia leaned forward slightly, looking Kassandra straight in the eye. "Before you say anything . . .Yes, I looked at your brother last time, and I..." Kassandra's gaze was interrogative as she looked at her: "You looked at who?" "Your brother." "Ooh okay." The young woman replied. "I didn't come here to talk to you about this, but it's good that you admit it...should I record it...?" she added sarcastically. She made a sort of grimace that was probably a smile for her. Cynthia felt partly relieved, thinking that the young woman wanted to confront her. She'd made a whole film about it. She waited for the rest of the discussion and leaned back comfortably in her seat. She motioned to Kassandra to continue. "I've actually come to see you because my brother would like to do a meeting with you. If you're up for it. Are you interested in him?" It was Cynthia's turn to look at her in amazement. She suddenly felt like dancing, jumping on the table and shouting "Yes! Of course!!!" She also wanted to hug 'cold' Kassandra. Instead, she played the mature, detached card. "Yes, I'm interested in him and would love to meet him insha'Allah." "Okay, honestly, I was reluctant to ask. Especially since you seem to have a relationship with this guy...» Cynthia interrupted her immediately : « I don't have a relationship with this guy, he's a former colleague. He just visited me without informing me » "I hope so." And Kassandra stood up, "I'll let my brother know that you are interested to meet him. Can you give me your number?"

She gave her number phone and watched Kassandra go outside to join her brother on the terrace. He looked at Cynthia. They smiled briefly at each other. The young man plunged back into his newspaper while quietly drinking his coffee. Then the girl saw her sister sitting down in front of him and talking. Cynthia walking on the air. Alhamdulillah! What a miracle! "If he asks to speak to me, it's because he likes me. She couldn't believe it. Why did he ask her? Did he know that all the girls in the group were after him? Had he already made another meeting? When she thought about it, she decided it would be wiser not to tell anyone (except Solena and Miriam, of course) until everything had been confirmed. The only question she asked herself was "Is he the one I'm looking for?" It seemed too good to be true and yet she wanted to believe it with all her heart. She thought that maybe he was, after all, he already matched several of the criteria on her list. And he seemed like a good person. She sipped her drink. She was over the moon. "Are you on your way to a reception or something?" Solena watched Cynthia trying on outfits, one by one. The young woman's bed was strewn with clothes. Nervous and stressed, she put on one hijab only to take it off and put on another. Kassandra had sent her a message to confirm the meeting that would take place this evening. In front of the mirror, none of them seemed to show her off enough. Finally, she went into the bathroom, splashed some fresh water on her face, and returned to the bedroom. She would wear her abaya, a long nude-colored dress, and a hijab of the same color. Then some lip balm. There was no need to do too much, she might as well show herself as it was the first time they met each other. The worst thing was to look like an Instagram filter... She really wanted to be dressed up and wearing make-up, tempted to cover her dark circles and brighten up her complexion, but she preferred to show him her everyday face so that he could be sure of who he was choosing.

"I'm going to tell you something. Don't tell anyone." "Alala Cynthia you're too mysterious. And then when you reveal your secrets..." Solena continued, signing imaginary commas, "It's like the bad fall of a joke " Then she laughed. "Very funny". Solena was her friend but what had just happened was so important, so improbable... But she knew her well. If she hadn't told her where she was going, she would have heard about it for centuries to come. She put on her shoes and led her friend to sit on the edge of the bed. Then, in a tone of confidence, she said: "I'm going to a marriage meeting later insha Allah". "With whom?" said Solena with a big smile of astonishment.

"It's just between us". "I promise insha Allah." Cynthia took a deep breath. "The tour guide... The girl who came to talk to us was her sister. She asked me if I was interested in her brother and if I'd be willing to meet him." Solena didn't give her time to say anything more. She hugged her and led her into a sort of dance of joy. "I'm super mega happy for you! Man, the other girls are going to die of jealousy, and I can't hide the fact that I would have liked to be in your place..." Then she added, "But I'm happy for you Alhamdulillah. You've been through so much. I hope from the bottom of my heart that it all ends well, insha'Allah, and may Allah make it easier for you, so hurry up and tell me all about it later!" Cynthia picked up her handbag and went outside. Her stomach was in knots. Because of her previous encounters, she knew what questions to ask. She was especially afraid of the answers. When she entered the prayer room, the brother and the imam were already there. They were sitting on the thick, luxurious carpet that covered the floor of the room. It was simple but spacious lit by the light through the large windows and the richly decorated lamps that adorned the walls and ceiling. At the end of the room was a large library filled with Quran and Tafseer's books. It was empty because it was not yet prayer time. The brother interrupted his discussion and looked up at her. Cynthia felt herself melting on the spot. The imam greeted her and sat down not far from them, leaving them to talk. "Salam aleykum.Thank you for coming." Cynthia could feel her heart beating a hundred miles an hour. "Wa 'aleykum salam. It's normal... you invited me" she replied, stammering. He smiled. "Make yourself comfortable Cynthia." "Okay" And she sat down, leaving a large space between them and facing her suitor. "So I was thinking that as our relationship has evolved, we could get to know each other a little better..." "Oh ? And how did it evolve?" The young woman laughed shyly... It was the first time she had seen him so well. She could see every detail of his face. He had such beautiful eyes and lips... macha Allah. She pulled herself together so as not to get distracted and concentrated

62

on what he was saying. He had a sense of humor, which was a good thing. It was so intriguing because it contrasted with his apparent seriousness. "I heard you admired my swimming skills... Cynthia thought back to Kassandra when she had come to find her at the top of the rocks. She was embarrassed, but now there was no need to worry about that. Weren't they here to get married? « Yes, that's true, she laughs. Your sister doesn't seem to like me very much. She said with a little smile." "Yes, but it doesn't matter. As far as I'm concerned, I like you." At these words, Cynthia felt a lot of butterflies in her stomach. She felt flattered but didn't dare look him in the face. It was better not to have too much hope. "Tell me about yourself he continued. And she talked about her studies, the job she'd just left, her parents, and the fact that she was very close to them. They formed a solid couple despite the ups and downs. Her father had contracted an illness that had forced him to

quit his job. As a result, her mother took over and worked as an administrative secretary at a secondary school. Her father was no less inactive; he could no longer run his recycling business alone, but he gave advice based on his experience as CEO on an online course platform.

She had an older sister whom she greatly admired and got on really well with. And a little sister who loved to get on her nerves but whom she loved more than anything. Cynthia was living in a small studio in Paris. In the near future, she hoped to make the hijra to a Muslim country and, why not, set up her own patisserie. As time went by, her tongue loosened. She felt at ease with this man. He was a good confidant because he listened intently. He sometimes interrupted her to ask questions or react when he had had a similar experience. As a result, Cynthia felt confident and at the same time intimidated by his personality and beauty. He exuded charisma and kindness. As she spoke, she didn't look directly at him, but she could feel his gaze on her. He asked her questions, always wanting to know more, and listened attentively to her answers. When it was his turn, he got straight to the point. He was born in Ireland. As a teenager, he went to a boarding school for young men in England. Then, as part of his studies, Liam had lived in France for a few years. Even physically, with his black hair and beard and tanned skin, he could easily have passed for an African or an Arab. His sister Kassandra, on the other hand, although very brunette, with her white skin, you could immediately see her Irish origins. His parents, who traveled a lot, finally settled in Oman to develop their hotel chain in the Emirates with his uncle. From there, the young man set up his own travel agency 4 years ago, shortly after converting to Islam. He had encountered many difficulties in setting up and developing his business. But through determination and hard work, he managed to achieve his goal. His agency was now recognized for its professionalism and the originality of its destinations. He joked that it was a good thing she hadn't filed a complaint, that it was the first time it had happened to them. "Yes, my heart's in the right place about that, I forgave you," Cynthia replied with a smile. When she asked him how he had converted, Liam became embarrassed. It was so cute how a man like him could be shy or embarrassed. "I promise I won't judge," she said, laughing. "I had my best friend who I often hung out with...We did a thing and he ended up in prison for a minor offense." Cynthia was curious; she found it hard to imagine Liam delinquent or hanging around with someone who was. Just goes to show, that you should never trust appearances... "Come on, say it all!" And she laughed. "I used to visit him at least once a month. But for a long time, I wasn't able to. Finally, one day, I went back to see him. He had changed a lot. At first, I thought it was because of the way he was treated, the environment, etc. But then I was not able to see him for fews months. This prison, Shelton Abbey, is more like a holiday resort... So that day, he told me about the Quran, about this Muslim guard with whom he had long spiritual discussions. He was passionate about it but refuted everything the guy told me. The following month, I came back and he

64

was a Muslim. It was a shock. Cynthia saw Liam's face blossom into a big smile as he remembered his friend. "It was surprising because my mate never believed in God. He even had a rather obscene tattoo on the back of his neck. Liam laughed. "Since then, he's had it removed. And you know, I remember that he was the first to criticize Islam and religions in general. And there he was, looking like he'd calmed down, all that rage he'd had inside him... nothing. He was a new man. Knowing that his family is very practicing, they're Catholics. And he was ready to tell them about his conversion. For me, it was a turning point". During his visits to the prison, he listened to his friend, at first taking him for a madman, and then their discussions raised questions. From there, Liam bought many books that finally convinced him. But it was when he read the Quran that he decided to convert to Islam. "It's been the best thing that's ever happened to me, and I you are the second, masha Allah," he added, smiling at Cynthia. The young woman was touched. They had only known each other for a few days, let's say even a few hours, and she felt irresistibly attracted to him. Not just physically, but as if he were her other half, her soul mate. She didn't want to end their conversation. She felt connected to the young man and could see how they were on the same page. It was just something wonderful that she had never experienced on her last date, or with Samuel! "It was a wonderful conversion story, masha Allah. "What about you?" asked Liam. "I'll tell you. My story is less interesting. It's a quick story. My father has Erithreans origins. He's not a Muslim. He's Catholic. There are a lot of Catholics in Eritrea. My mother is mixed white and Senegalese. But it is the same, she is catholic. We have some of members of our family who converted to Islam but I mainly learn by hanging out with Muslim friends. It interested me, so I started reading books too and here I am. My parents support me and that's all that is important to me. » Liam and Cynthia began exchanging the titles of books they had read on their spiritual journey. She was pleased that he confided in her. For her, it was a sign that she could trust him.

They continued the discussion, talking about what they expected from married life. They asked each other questions. She was intrigued that a man who seemed so accomplished still wasn't married. So she asked him. To which he replied quite honestly. "It took me a long time to find myself. I used to be a party boy and my life was unstable for quite a while before I converted. And then, with the creation of my business, I didn't really have the time to make plans for marriage even I wanted to or meet interesting people". Cynthia smiled, "So I'm an interesting person?" The brother replied seriously, "Yes, the first one. yes the first in a long time as soon as I saw you." He added with a beautiful smile. "Where the hell am I? It's like another dimension of Wattpad. It was too good to be true??" how to explain what she was feeling right now? She felt appreciated, wanted, desired... it was a little overwhelming, so much so that she had waited and was discovering her « person » in Liam. It was not a movie...It was the actual reality.

She told him about her personal journey to get married, and she told her encounters from worst to best. "Well, lately, I was on 'Myhalallove,'" Liam confided. Cynthia exclaimed with surprise. "Me too! And you didn't find it?" "No, I stayed for a few hours and then deleted my account." They both agreed that old- fashioned dating was much better. They were both at ease. She listened avidly to his words. It still amazed her that they got on so well and had so much in common. Time flew by and he would no doubt have continued if the imam hadn't got up to perform the adhan. After the salat, the imam was happy for them that their exchange had gone well. He gave a reminder in Arabic and English about the importance of marriage and not to waste time. Liam undertook to translate for her. Cynthia knew a bit of literary Arabic in terms of reading, and she perfectly understand and speaking English. She was impressed that Liam knew so many language. This was another characteristic she admired in the young man. He invited her to come and stay with her sister at their house. "I won't be staying with you. But I would like you and my sister to get to know each other insha'Allah. What do you say?" She would have liked to tell him that she preferred to stay away from Kassandra but she couldn't say no to him. Besides... It wasn't such a bad idea. At least it would allow her to get to know her future sister-in-law better. The appointment was made. She and her sister would meet this evening to go to the house. When she returned to her room, Solena was waiting for her, lying on her bed in her bathrobe. Her face was covered with a greenish beauty mask. "Madame is back! ahaha" she exclaimed as she straightened up. "Olàlà, I can't take it anymore, please tell me everything!" "At least wait until I've changed..." "Ah, no ma'am. I know you, it's going to take you 100,000 years to get over that. I would have had time to start a family...Again". Cynthia laughed. She sat down on the bed and spilled the beans about her meeting with the brother. "Can you see my sister? I told you. Allah is in charge of everything Alhamdulillah." "Or wait, I'll wait until you get married insha'Allah and then it will be my turn insha'Allah. I'm sure he has connections," she said with a falsely serious face. They called Miriam to share the news. Cynthia felt again over the moon. Her long wait had finally been rewarded. And she felt happy and comforted to be surrounded by her two friends who had always been there for her. Miriam also had some news: she was getting married. Her mother and aunt had found her a young man of Bangladeshi origin who came from a good Muslim family and lived in England. Miriam was also of Bangladeshi origin, but her family was not against her marrying a man of another origin. The main thing for them was religion. And this was also the case for Miriam. She talked a lot with her aunts and her mother. Because of their experiences and the divorces she had witnessed, the young woman decided to involve them in her search for a husband. When her mother told her she was going to marry her off, the young woman didn't object. She truly believed that the old-fashioned methods were the best, especially for today's young Muslims who were encountering more difficulties in finding their better half. Her friends did not judge her, far from it, and supported her too. "Girls...? Solena raised her arms to the sky. I can feel that it's my turn soon, insha'Allah. There are too many signs here! Cynthia hugged her friend. "And she pressed a kiss to the top of her head to avoid her beauty mask. "Wow, that smells weird. What's in the mask?" Solena looked mysterious. "I don't give my beauty secrets for free darling, you'll get yours the day before your wedding insha'Allah!"

Chapter 11

The ring of discord

Allah says: (Those who do not invoke other Gods with Allah Those who do not destroy a soul, as it is protected by Allah from a ban; those who abstain from fornication, for whoever commits fornication encounter a major sin; those who abstain from fornication, for whoever commits fornication encounter a major sin: Allah will increase his torment on the Day of Resurrection. Except for those who repent, believe, and do good deeds; for them, Allah substitutes good deeds for their evil deeds, for God is All-Forgiving, All-Merciful]

[S.25, V.68-70]

The room was bathed in soft, subdued light. Outside, you could hear the waves crashing against the rocks. Cynthia watched the man she loved, who was now her husband, approached her. He was literally kissing her with his eyes. "After all we've been through, I'm happy to be able to be with you at last, Cynthia...and...I've loved and wanted you since the first day I saw you..." She felt his hands run up her arms and stop on her shoulders. Gently, with his fingertips, he removed the satin jacket, which slid down to her ankles, And under his ardent kisses, Cynthia felt the desire to take hold of her...

Cynthia joined Kassandra in a luxury car. She'd never seen one like it except in ads or films. Their driver was none other than Liam, who had changed for the occasion. He was wearing a polo shirt and mid-length shorts. His eyes were hidden by aviator- style glasses. He was really classy. After opening the door for them, he got behind the wheel of the car. "Please bring us back safely," Kassandra said sarcastically. "I'll try insha'Allah. I suggest you get your driving licence so you can drive your own car." "I don't know where these rumors are coming from, you know very well I've got it! Don't damage it. Thank you!". Inside, Cynthia was comfortably seated, her back pressed into the leather seat. The windows were tinted. Except for the roof window, which showed a starry sky. The journey was silent. About an hour later, Liam pulled up in front of an imposing ultra- modern building. He opened the door for them and Cynthia gazed in wonder at their home. But she refrained from sharing her impressions. Inside, the furniture was sleek and modern. Well, I'll leave you to it," Liam told them from the car, "I'm going for a ride and I'll see you later, insha'Allah." "And please be careful. It's a present from dad. If you scratch my car, I'll kill you Liam." He gave her a little "yes boss" sign and sped off. "I'm going to kill him," whispered Kassandra as she watched the car pull away. "Come on, I'll take you on a tour of the house."

Kassandra turned to Cynthia. "If you get married, you'll come here on holiday, it's the family home but also a holiday home. Our main residence is in Ireland, so we don't stay there much." She said. "I've never seen her more arrogant, what a contrast with her brother! Cynthia thought inwardly. And they went from room to room. The style was refined and modern. The furniture was Danish style, Ikea in level 10 mode. She saw the huge living room. In one part, there was a creamy white sofa, very cozy, opposite a fake fireplace, the carpet in the same tone as the sofa, made you want to roll around in it. The floor was covered in marble. Further along was a large dining table with at least 8 chairs on either side. Cynthia noticed that there was no television screen. "Don't expect to live in luxury, Liam is very...let's just say he lives simply. She looked at her with slight disdain. "But I suppose even his 'simple' will change your life," she said with a big smile "I have no idea what he sees in you". Cynthia replied slightly annoyed "I'm used to simplicity, you see, and believe me, I'd rather be surrounded by people I like than surrounded by furniture, depressed and....Alone," She added with a condescending tone, looking at the young woman from head to toe. She could see that Kassandra had taken the remark personally. Cynthia continued "And...Maybe I just have qualities that he likes and admires". Kassandra pretended to choke. "We're both Muslims, how about some good behavior? You're a convert too, you should learn to behave a bit." Said Cynthia. The woman didn't seem at all impressed. She leaned against the wall. "I'll be honest with you. Liam is my twin brother, and I have to admit that he has a lot of qualities that make it easy for women to approach him. I've seen it all and even though I'm a woman, I've lost all faith in them. Between the ones who are married, the ones who chase him for his money... I don't want him to make a mistake. He's come a long way, he doesn't need to suffer anymore.

Cynthia felt compassion for Kassandra. She finally has a heart... "And frankly I don't understand why he chose you, you don't come from our world, so your intentions...I don't trust it. You can be sure that I won't make it easy for you." ...A heart of ice. Cynthia had believed it, but in the end, she was right about her first impression of this girl. "First of all, I'd like to point out that it wasn't me who took the first step towards him. Alhamdulillah," she added emphatically. "Secondly, I like your brother very much. I like him for his qualities and honestly... I can see myself making babies with him." "Yuck." Kassandra let out, which disconcerted Cynthia. "Nah, but making babies in the literal sense of the word, I don't talk about...er, I...What I want to tell is..." "Akward, Akward. Please, girl, be quiet." Kassandra said with an air of disdain. « If you're hungry, we can go down to the kitchen. We'll keep your mouth busy before you start talking too much nonsense. I haven't got enough aspirin for my head." "It's not her you're going to marry insha Allah, but her brother, breaathe" Cynthia thought. "Alhamdulillah, I'm ambitious. I've got a degree and I intend to work and earn my own money. I'm definitely not after his... your money," she resumed. "Okay, I have to say you're convincing. So I'll give you the benefit of the doubt. But you won't get rid of me with a wave of your magic wand, I'm here to look after Liam. And sorry, but you don't seem to be his Princess." She reapplied a layer of pink lip balm. Cynthia saw the word Givenchy on the tube. "Maybe the pumpkin?" She added, opening her eyes exaggeratedly. And she laughed wickedly. "Have you thought about getting treatment?" Cynthia retorted, asking her in all seriousness. She was hurt by such aggression, but she refrained from showing it. She didn't want to give her that gift. Kassandra turned to her: "Maybe if you go, I won't even need it," she replied in the same tone. "Brilliant! I'll have a completely crazy sister-in-law!

The two girls went downstairs into the ultra-modern kitchen. Which was twice the size of his modest studio apartment. Cynthia particularly noticed the large worktops, which could hold a lot of things and were reminiscent of a kitchen workshop. There were two huge fridges with built-in screens, and one had a water dispenser. the place was clean and all the surfaces shiny, it was easy to think that the kitchen was rarely used. They ate the sushi that Kassandra had ordered. Although it wasn't euphoria, they did manage to talk about various subjects, including religion. "I need you to be honest. Was this man really your colleague? At this point, Cynthia felt completely drained. What was she supposed to say? No, but he was in the bedroom and we more or less kissed...??" Confiding in this witch was out of the question. Cynthia didn't know how it would be interpreted or how it would be used. But it was clear that it would be to her disadvantage. If she had to talk about it, it would be only to Liam. "Have you seen my ring?" "...you're still wearing?" finished Kassandra with disdain. "Yes, I can see it, and I don't understand why you still have it on your finger if it's really over. I think you should focus on the man who gave you that ring and do everything you can to keep him. A proposal, followed by a ring, is a clear sign of love." Just then, Liam made his entrance, interrupting the moment of unease. In good mood, he didn't even notice the tension between the 2 women. "Time to go home Cynthia. I hope my sister didn't scare you too much?" he added with a smirk. "Yes. I do, I'm scared for our future. She needs to be locked up, she's a danger to humanity." But she simply replied, "Yes, a little bit. Is she under the influence... ? ". Liam laughed. If he only knew! She voluntarily climbed into the back of the car. She could feel Liam's attraction to her. His eyes said a thousand things that she knew he was restraining himself from telling her. And ever since their meeting in the mosque, she couldn't help but feel the same. The journey in the car was silent. But when they passed a date plantation, Liam stopped. « I know these farmers. They're friends of mine. Would you like to wait for me ?» He got out of the car and she saw him running towards a man who greeted her with a big smile. They greeted each other. He was dressed in a qamis and wearing a turban. Around him were baskets filled with dates. Cynthia went outside to admire the scenery. Leaning against the car. When she saw Liam returning in the distance, carrying a large plastic bag, she got back into the car. I met this man when I moved here. One day I was passing by and he ended up inviting me regularly to eat at his and his family's house. I help him by exporting his dates abroad, so that he has more income. We're business partners. He took out a large, shiny, fresh date and handed it to her from his seat. "The bag is for you. »

Cynthia couldn't help smiling "Thank you! May Allah reward you". She picked up the bag. "I've got dates for the next few months!" she laughed. When we're married, insha'Allah, I'd like to introduce you to them. They're like a second family. The Omanis are very warm and welcoming people. It's also one of the things that made me love this country. » When they arrived in front of the hotel, he parked the car, got out and opened the door for her. "What a gentleman," thought the young woman.

Liam stood in front of her. "I can't wait for us to spend more time together insha'Allah." He said all this as he took the bag from her hand. "Let's get inside. I'll drop this off on your doorstep. "I'm not a fragile little thing you know ?I can carry a bag of, let's say...a kilo of dates " She said ironically.

"I know you're not. It's just that it gives me an excuse to go with you." He added confidently. They made their way to his room. He set the bag down in front of the door and left. Not without giving her a smile. Back in her room, she thought back to her tête-à-tête with Kassandra. That girl was awful ! Thinking about it, Cynthia was upset

. Not from sadness, but from anger at being treated like a nobody. Like shit, in fact. She was on edge. "How can he have such a sister! Oh my God, what a nightmare!" She had found the right man, she was sure of it. But because of her sister, she was afraid that everything would fall through. In the semi- darkness, she looked down at her hand, where Samuel's wedding ring was shining. Kassandra was at least right about one thing: a ring is a sign of attachment. Should she really reproach her for his lack of trust, when she was wearing a ring given to her by a man? Seen from the outside, this mistake did call into question her sincerity towards Liam. But in truth, it was just a faux-pas. She'd tried the ring on, found it pretty, and simply forgotten to take it off. There was something else: having met Liam, she realized another obvious fact: she didn't like Samuel. She didn't feel in harmony with him, she didn't feel comfortable in his presence. She didn't feel connected to him. She took off the ring. And texted the young man: "I've made my decision. I'm sorry to have wasted your time but we're not going to continue. Please don't call me again. I'll give you your ring back when I get back to Paris insha'Allah." Liam was the only person she wanted to be with now.Even though everything seemed to be happening so quickly, they had a lot in common. Their hearts seemed bound together. In his presence, she felt safe and at peace. Was it the meaning of soulmate? The next morning, a reminder was organised by a mu'alima from the town. The men, for their part, had been given a lecture by the imam on the importance of remembering Allah. Solena and Cynthia were really enthusiastic. The trip was also an opportunity to revitalise their faith. The reminder was about the choices we are led to make during trials. It was translated from Arabic into French. The girls were seated in a conference room. A woman in her fifties, maybe more, was seated at a table in front of the audience. In front of her was a microphone. Sitting next to her was a woman doing the translation. In the studious silence, his voice could be heard echoing. "...The Shaytan will always be in your way to lead you to perdition. He will embellish things for you." "Did he not say: "Because

74

You led me astray, I will stand in Your way to lead them astray. Then I will come to them from in front, from behind, on their right, and on their left. You will find a few of them grateful."

(S: 7/A: 16 and 17).

The speaker continued: "When you feel that you are about to slip, remember also that Iblis has promised that he will make us embellish evil". And she began to recite another verse of the Quran in Arabic and then, what the translator recited in French: "I will certainly lead them astray, fill them with false hopes, incite them to split the ears of cattle and I will incite them to change the creation of Allah." **(S: 4 /A: 119).** "Allah will always show you the signs of what is good or bad for you. If you remember Allah in everything you do, the Shaytan will have no hold on you." By the end of the reminder, Cynthia was more confident than ever in her decision to end her relationship with Samuel. No more false hope. Solena and Cynthia met the group at the hotel reception. Today they were to visit several tourist sites in Muscat. They were especially excited to see the Sultan Qaboos Grand Mosque. As Cynthia chatted with her friend, she was astonished to see Samuel enter the hotel with a big rose bouquet. He was dressed in a linen shirt and trousers and carrying a large messenger shoulder bag. He was as handsome as ever, full of confidence and smiling, but something had changed in the expression on his face. He appeared determined.Their eyes met. She and Solena saw him clip a small microphone to his collar, then he raised his smartphone as if to take a selfie and with astonishment they heard him say: "Today I'm going to ask the girl I love to marry me, wish me luck! Then they saw him tapping away on his phone, presumably to post. Solena began to giggle, "I can feel something epic coming on", as Samuel approached a table of tourists. He asked one of them to film him. Cynthia realised what he was about to do and was about to disappear, clinging to Solena's arm when she heard her name: « CYNTHIA! » Samuel ran across the space separating them from each other before the astonished eyes of the customers, waiters and other members of staff. The two girls turned around. Samuel knelt down in front of the embarrassed young woman. Somewhere in the back of her mind, Cynthia remembered how Solena and she used to laugh when they saw this kind of scene on social networks. "While this memory echoed in her head, she took the bouquet of roses that Samuel held out to her. Solena restrained herself from bursting out laughing. As soon as she saw the tourist acting as cameraman pointing his phone at them, she moved away. "Girl, I'm sorry but you're gonna have to handle this on your own..."

"I travelled miles to find you. Who would have thought that I, Samuel Karim, would fall madly in love? I can tell you that you've made a new man of me... and I want to announce it to the world, or more precisely to my 3,200 followers and the customers present", a few people laughed. Nervous, he breathed in and out as if to give himself strength, then turned to the small crowd.

"Ladies and gentlemen, I love this beautiful girl" Most were also filming the scene, he turned to Cynthia "I want you to share my life... Will you marry me?" Solena looked at them, with other sisters around her, as if it were a scene from a film, devouring her packet of crisps, with a bemused smile, half mocking, half impressed by the young man's courage.

It was a bold move on his part... But frankly, Cynthia regretted that he had decided to make this moment public. She wasn't really the type to expose her life on social media. And right now, all the young woman wanted to do was disappear. She could feel all the cameras riveted on her, scrutinising her reaction.

"Can we talk about this in private?" she said with a tense smile. Samuel sensed her embarrassment and immediately stood up. Signalling in "it's dead" mode to the tourist involved, as if it were a report, to cut the Instagram live.

He hadn't wasted any time! "Had he gone back to France or...had he spent his whole stay in the country?" Cynthia didn't know where to put herself. This was not the time to attract attention, especially with that witch Kassandra! She turned her head and saw that Liam was also looking at Samuel, torn between questioning and something else, that she couldn't guess. "Your ex-husband's here." Cynthia turned to face Kassandra, who seemed to be enjoying the scene. The young woman chose to ignore her. She had to send Samuel away. She looked again at Liam, who was now staring at her intently. Finally, he looked busy and indifferent again and continued his task with the group of tourists.

Cynthia nervously readjusted her veil and took Samuel aside while the people who were still smiling at the scene went back to what they were doing. "Thank you for your gesture, it means a lot to me... but why are you here?

"Isn't it obvious? Samuel held her gaze for a long moment before answering: "I don't understand your decision, who are you leaving me for?" He leaned back in his chair. He looked devastated. Cynthia refrained from answering. "I don't understand it. I thought we could get married...I've made a lot of efforts in the meantime." "Like what?" replied Cynthia. "I've left a lot behind." "Don't do it for me. Otherwise, it's worthless. I don't want you to change for me, Samuel. What I want is someone who shares my values. Without forcing yourself but want to do it with conviction." The young man was taken aback. He leaned over: "Listen, I'm not just doing this for you. My father is seriously ill.That opened my eyes to a lot of things. I'm a total mess. And now I find out that the only woman I love, the one I'm committed to, is leaving me...By text message? Are you serious? You couldn't even call?" Cynthia suddenly felt guilty and ashamed, but then she pulled herself together. "I'm sorry about your father. May Allah grant him a quick recovery. I know that you care a lot about him and that you're very close of him macha Allah. But as for our supposed engagement, it never happened. We weren't even together at first. We just talked about meeting up again to ask each other some questions but then...Our last discussion, I thought I had made myself clear about us. I'm sorry for the way it ended." "I need you, Cycy." She looked at him. Samuel's face was ravaged by sadness. And he looked suddenly tired. "Marry me. Then we won't have to stay away from each other." When two people love each other, they can overcome anything together. You know I can take care of you...I may not be perfect...but I love you." Cynthia felt sorry for him and guilty. He seemed sincere. She remembered what she had liked about him. His kindness and always in a good mood. But fortunately, she also remembered their very last conversation and how it had ended.

"What have you done with your ring?" "I put it away." "Okay, I got a room. You won't have to talk to me. But..." He paused to pay the bill and leave a tip. "...Don't give up on me like that. Just take some time to think please." And he stood up. Headed straight for the lift. Cynthia was nailed to her chair. He really wanted to be with her. Just when she thought she was moving on and imagined herself at Liam's side, Samuel came back, more determined than ever. Worse still he was moving in... here. She got up suddenly to run behind him but he had already rushed into the lift. She entered quickly. "Please don't say anything to anyone." "Say what? Samuel said sarcastically. And he approached her. Looking at her with gentleness. "To say that I'm madly in love with you? He didn't give her time to reply. He touched her cheek with delicacy with his fingertips. "Or that something almost happened between you and me?" He lifted her chin, forcing her to look at him. "Cycy?" "Nothing's happened," begged the young woman. "I'm afraid of the consequences if you talk." "If you marry me, you won't have to worry about what people think and I would never do anything to harm you.You should know that." He left her there, dejected, while people rushed to her. The lift doors closed. She pressed the button leading to the reception desk. Cynthia could feel problems coming...

Chapter 12

Complication and Tears

"There are people who worship Allah while being disturbed and if something good happens to them, their hearts are appeased by it and ifever a catastrophe happens to them, they turn away from faith", [surat al- Hajj / 11]. "And trust in Allah if you are believers" [**Surat al- ma'idah /23**]

Samuel was sitting on a sofa on the hotel terrace. There were a few residents. "Foreigners, he thought, probably Americans. One of them was staring at him. At first he ignored her, but she and her girlfriends seemed to be trying to get his attention by talking and laughing loudly. "Not my type." No, his type was Cynthia and she was pushing him away. He'd never had a problem seducing a woman. In fact, he'd never been rejected. He'd never thought about settling down until he met Cynthia. She was so...sweet and cute in her way. Well okay, as a guy it wasn't what he noticed first. Before they worked together, he did not hesitate to stare at her when she was busy. She always made sure to cover herself, loose trousers, long skirts. But all her efforts to hide did not make her less desirable. He took pleasure even in guessing his shapes to imagine how she was. Yes, we can say that he was really attracted to her. She had a pretty mouth, which she used to bite when upset or stressed. Several times he had wanted to kiss her, he wanted her to be his. And He thought that she had pretty eyes. And when she lifted them on him to ask him something, he felt at the center of the world. He was happy to have her attention even for the most futile thing. He could not help but want to take her in his arms. He thought she was beautiful, intelligent, and determined in everything she did. And kind, yes, that was what had marked him when he was working alongside her. She naturally helped those around her, even if it meant sacrificing a little of her time. Very empathetic, she took the time to listen to you. This evening at the factory, he realized that he was in love. It was the first time he'd felt that kind of attachment to a girl.

That was beyond sexual attraction. He wanted more. Like knowing her, hanging out with her. Listening to her voice all day. And for him, her religion, her veil, nothing seemed to be an obstacle to a possible love story... But she had pulled away, then fled. When she cut off all contact and put radical distances between them, it didn't stop him from still caring about her. Honestly, he didn't know if he was really ready for marriage. He just wanted to be with Cynthia and if that was what she wanted, he was ready to commit. You don't give up on love that easily, and he had gone to great lengths to be able to find her here. Except that he had behaved like an idiot. If he'd known that their one kiss would be another reason for his estrangement, he would have abstained... But Cynthia provoked so many things in him that it was a real test. He was obsessed with her. He had always chosen one-night stands. The notion of commitment had always frightened him. But with her... he'd broken that barrier. Right now, no other woman interested him. He finished his glass of juice. He didn't drink alcohol. "But it takes a lot more than that to win her over, mate" he said to himself. His relationship with religion was complex. His father was a religious man, but even if Samuel saw him praying or fasting during Ramadan, it really seemed cultural to him. Sometimes he went on holiday to visit the family in Marocco. Sometimes he went to the mosque on Fridays and fasted during Ramadan because he knew it was compulsory. But then, like many other young Muslims of his generation, he didn't feel involved enough to make religious practice a permanent part of his life. Until he met Cynthia. For her, he was ready to make an effort and get involved. He was able to confide in her. The fact that their fathers were affected by the disease had brought them both closer. They exchanged news and encouraged each other. They both had the same ambitions in life and the same love of baking. She was his perfect wife..."You seem very lonely..." A female voice drew him from his thoughts. In front of him was a sister with a cold stare. She was beautiful but definitely not friendly. Her face was familiar. I'm waiting for someone." "Are you

80

sure? Because you've been sitting there for a while..." He put down his empty glass. And leaned against his back. "Do you need anything?" The young woman was facing him. "I'm the one who called you...I'm Kassandra. We spoke on the phone about my brother and...your friend." At these words, Samuel remembered the call he had received from a woman. So it was Kassandra... It was this woman who had told him about Cynthia's plans to marry. About the meeting that had taken place between her and her brother. She didn't want him to marry her. So they had something in common. Following their discussion, the man wasted no time. He took the first flight to put an end to Cynthia's plans and remind her of his love for her.

But with hindsight, he realized that he was associating with someone diabolical. Kassandra was prepared to stand in the way of her own brother's happiness...but also that of the woman he loved without worrying about the harm she would do. Samuel wondered if he really had to go on. He loved Cynthia deeply and wanted to be with her. There was no denying that. But not to the point of breaking her heart and ruining her life. "I'll talk to you later," Kassandra murmured and she walked away quickly. He didn't know whether he should agree to talk to her, go back home to France or just... He saw Cynthia. He felt a surge of emotion. She had a book in her arms and was moving towards a lounge chair. She hadn't seen him until now. He hailed the waiter and ordered a second drink, a non- alcoholic cocktail, which he sipped as he watched Cynthia. He wouldn't go to her tonight, even though he was dying to talk to her and explain. In the lift, he had sensed that she needed to think and to have some space. He feared that if he put too much pressure on her, she might run away again. He would have to be patient. She was also the only one who could understand him because his own father was ill. He needed her comfort so badly, he needed to talk to her... "Women..." It was the first time he'd ever felt so pathetic. Cynthia made herself comfortable on the chaise longue. Deep down she was hoping to bump into Liam, whom she hadn't seen all day.

Her conversation with Samuel had left a bitter taste in her mouth and she hadn't been able to think of anything other than the catastrophe that would happen if Liam ever found out what kind of relationship she'd had with her supposed 'ex- husband'. With her gaze, she scanned the pool. "Why aren't you here? Cynthia thought sadly. "Maybe he's changed his mind about me."

She remembered with nostalgia their first meeting, and when he had spoken to her for the first time. The time they had spent talking... Beautiful memories that she still hoped to relive. She stood up.

Rest was better than spending the evening brooding. When she entered the hotel, she saw Liam. Backpack and sunglasses on his nose. She felt herself melting. He was dressed all in white. Wearing mid-length trousers and a polo shirt that revealed a firm, muscular torso. He was handling some equipment, which he placed behind the reception desk.She made a timid wave with her hand, but he didn't seem to notice, and he continued towards the lift. Cynthia lowered her hand. Suddenly sad. "He didn't see me... or didn't want to see me. . . " She waited a moment, watching the neon numbers on the lift scroll by. Then she walked, suddenly discouraged, to the lift, into which she entered. She thought she would have to clear things up with Samuel. There was no way she was going to ruin everything because of misunderstandings. Besides, she owed him an explanation. He deserved at least that. When she entered the room, she found Solena lying on her bed, her eyes red with tears. She rushed towards her. "Can you tell me what's bothering you? Why are you crying? Have you heard from your children?" Solena straightened up, sitting down on the bed. "Yes, don't worry, they're fine, Al- Hamdulillah. It's nothing to do with that.» "What's the problem with you then?" Solena showed her the conversation she just had with a brother on the "MyHalallove" application. The conversation had got off to a good start. It was Solena who had taken the initiative to contact the brother whose profile was attractive. Like her, he had 2 children, was divorced. He was in his thirties. In his photo, he was quite handsome. Bald as an egg, but attractive. Cynthia could see straight away what Solena was looking for. The brother had a beautiful smile and in his description, he seemed funny and kind. He had said "You shouldn't judge people with children" and Cynthia quoted aloud, "We all have a past and I'm not going to stop there. I'm just looking for my other half, my best friend. If this sounds like you, contact me!"

Then he and Solena exchanged photos. To which the brother replied that she was really beautiful. Which was not untrue. This girl had a face and a body, in Cynthia's opinion, that took her breath away. And neither Miriam nor Cynthia understood the difficulties she was having in rebuilding her life. Next, the brother asked how many children she had, and if she could give their ages, which of course Solena did. As soon as she answered, the brother ghosted her. Barely a second later, he 'un-matched' her. "What a coward. I'm going to stay polite..."Cynthia was furious to see such behavior. "You've already given him a chance because believe me, not many women would have accepted a bald, unemployed man!" Solena laughed, then cried harder. "He is creator content ! »Cynthia looked at her friend. « *My* sister is creator content, until one day she becomes famous, for the moment she earns absolutely nothing. We are all content creator actually, sis ». Solena sniffed, then blew her nose « As soon as I say I've got kids, they either ghost me or tell me there are too many. Why can't these men see beyond that?" Cynthia sat down next to her friend. "Because, quite simply, they're not men. I'm talking, of course, about those who treat you like shit because of that. If they were worth it, they'd at least behave themselves. They're not ready to take responsibility, maybe some of them just want to have fun." "In the end, they're doing you a favor. You mustn't feel guilty or belittled because of this situation. You or your kids are not the problem, you just need to find the right person insha Allah. A man who's ready to live with the wonderful woman you are and your wonderful children. Some women have rebuilt their lives with many more children!" Solena blew her nose loudly, "Oh yes, which ones?" Cynthia continued,

"Well, for a start, remember the Prophet (ﷺ).He married Khadija (radhi ʿala ʿanha) who had already been married twice and had one or 3 children from her first marriage from what I've read on the subject. It's supposed to be an example. THIS is the example that the men of our community should follow. If those you've met haven't understood that, it's all right, Solena. » « Ô girl! I love you but right now I need more recent examples..." ? » Said Solena.

Cynthia looking thoughtful: « The one who deserves you and who will really be a man will come to you, don't worry". "Some people aren't afraid of marrying a woman with children because they know they'll be able to look after them financially and everything else..." Then Solena looked at the young woman and said: "I'm not even asking for that much, you know. I don't expect a man to look after my children ! I already do that. And even if their father behaves disgustingly towards me, he's there for them." » She blew her nose loudly.

Then got up to throw the tissue she had into the bedroom bin and pulled another from the packet before sitting back down. "Nah, I just want company Cynthia. I want to love, to be loved, to know love after being in a miserable relationship for years. I'm not into the whole "Oh, rebuild yourself, find happiness on your own, be happy on your own so you can be happy with someone else" thing anymore. That kind of talk bores me now. Solena was no longer crying, but her friend could see that the sadness was still there: "I've had time to rebuild myself, to make my own way and now I want to get married again. Do you think it is easy not to give into temptation? If I listened to myself, I would have remade my life with the first man coming or or I would have slept with anybody." She laughed but was bitter... She continued: "Sorry, I don't want to ruin our holiday, it's just that I'm a bit cracked at the moment." Cynthia took her in her arms. "You don't have to apologize, I understand you. I feel the same loneliness and the same need as you.But

I definitely can't compare my situation to yours. "Oh, no. It's all the same, don't diminish the burden you have compared to me. We're all tested at our level." Cynthia understood what the young woman meant about rebuilding herself. She had seen her change from a woman who had been the victim of domestic violence to the woman she is today, confident and happy. It was only natural that she should now want to settle down again.

Solena sighed. "It's just, you know, coming here, being without my children, I've got more time for myself and to feel my situation... And I had high hopes too when I signed up for "Myhalallove" Cynthia clapped her hands. Restraining herself from adding that she had warned her. "So you admit it's a waste of time? For the first time since they'd been talking, Solena began to smile. "No! I also think that these apps should be a bit more supervised. This one has an admin, but it's a shame that profiles are not checked and sorted. The tool itself isn't a waste of time, it's the men I've spoken to who are." "It's all the same," said Cynthia. "No, not at all. I work on the principle that this application is an intermediary like any other. It's just that compared to real life, the percentage of toads is higher. I could have met the same profiles outside this app." She looked at her friend, who didn't seem convinced. "I respect your choice, Solena. About me, I have already deleted it from my phone. I think it's too superficial." "I'd like you to read my book... Shall we have a "Gone with the Love" evening? The two girls laughed. Cynthia was happy to see her friend smile again. They both watched Islamic reminders on the tests in life and then lay down on the bed to read the rest of the Romance novel. *"Never! They can take my motorbike, but they'll never take you away from me!" Astafara wanted to cry. What a man! Not only he was a billionaire, Alpha man, but he also had a heart in Gold." She wanted him to remove her hijab and grasp her hair and kiss her fiercely, but he had to marry her first. She was going to pray all night for his release. Except... his heart was divided between him and Franco. "Say no more!". She told him. The prison doors* closed on Antonio. *"Baby boo, you will always my Omega"* He said to her. *He was so virile! "Antoniooooo!", cried out the young woman, tears streaming down her jaws. She fainted.*

Solena and Cynthia look at each other: "Girl...?" Started Solena "Yeah. Yeah...I know. It is really, really bad."

Chapter 13

The Princess and the Toads

Abu Hurairah (May Allah be pleased with him) reported: Messenger of Allah (ﷺ), "The believers who show the most perfect Faith are those who have the best behavior, and the best of you are those who are the best to their wive."

At-Tirmidhi, who categorized it as Hadith Hasan Sahih]

Abu Huraira reported that: The Prophet of Allah (ﷺ)said,"Treat women nicely, for a women is created from a rib, and the most curved portion of the rib is its upper portion, so, if you should try to straighten it, it will break, but if you

leave it as it is, it will remain crooked. So treat women nicely."

[Al- Bukhaari and Muslim]

Solena had refrained from telling Cynthia the real reason why she was crying. Not that she didn't trust her friend, far from it! But she didn't want to worry her. Shortly before her friend returned to the room, Solena had had a long chat with her ex via text message. The man had a talent for turning her mood around in 2 seconds. She had left him, it's true. But the imprint he had left on her was still there. She was marked by all those years of a toxic relationship. Years of hearing that she was worthless, that she was nothing. She had been ashamed to tell Miriam and Cynthia, and especially her family. She didn't see much of them at the time because of an argument, a bad word from her, or the mood of the moment any excuse was good enough to cancel her plans, even if they had been prepared months or weeks in advance. If she rebelled, her mobile phone would be confiscated. Later, the young woman confided to Miriam that when she saw people, it was as if there was a thick pane of glass between her and them. She could see but not hear them, they weren't part of her world. And she was not a part of their world. During those years, Solena lived in darkness. The psychological violence she suffered led her to develop speech impediments. She began to stutter, and often forgot what she wanted to say. "Shut your mouth"; Who told you to speak? Shut up". In the end, she adapted so well that she no longer knew who she was. What was worse?" It was the people around this man. Family and friends, close or otherwise, turned a blind eye to the physical and psychological abuse she suffered and minimized. This entourage only knew the sympathetic version of his ex. The funny, helpful version. And who turned a blind eye to the rest. Far from Miriam and Cynthia, this entourage had become her own. Among them, she had a 'friend' whom she confided in because their husbands were the best of friends. "Oh, don't worry. I'm going through it too. Last time, he shouted at me..." Solena had felt neither listened to nor heard, his suffering had been minimized. She quickly stopped talking. People don't like to hear disturbing things that make them feel uncomfortable and disrupt their daily lives. "Everything's fine" was her new mask, which she tried to wear for the rest of her marriage. Years later, she would bump into this girl, smiling and sweet as honey, but who couldn't hide the judgment in her eyes? Before Solena left her ex, Henry, there was already a rift between the two women. Because their husbands were so close, Solena had decided not to confide in each other for a long time. And yes, she was still thinking about preserving her husband's image. The man who was making her miserable. And even when she decided to leave, she said nothing. It all clicked when she realized that if she was going to survive, she had to leave. Henry had said to her after one of their many arguments: "Finally, you're more resourceful than you look. I must say you're brave".

Hearing it from her aggressor had given her the final push to leave. She told him about the divorce, took a few things and her children, and left for Miriam's place, who agreed to put her up for a while until she could get back on her feet. It had taken her a century to rebuild herself. She concentrated on her two children, literally living only for them, looking after their well-being. At 21, while her friends were thinking about shopping and going to the cinema, she had no time to relax. She had to work. Fortunately, her family was there to support her through thick and thin, but she didn't want her children to suffer from her new situation as a single mother. She hadn't saved them from a toxic environment so that they would still be in a precarious situation! At the age of 23, she had found a flat again, she had a part-time job as a virtual assistant, and on top of the benefits, that was enough to cover her rent, and her bills and look after her children. Her faith had been a great help to her, helping her to keep things in perspective in the face of hard times. Little by little, she regained her happiness, surrounding her children with her maternal love, and watching them blossom in an environment filled with love and laughter. Even if without lying it wasn't always easy, but she was happy to see them happy. She was enjoying the time with her family and her two best friends again. Sometimes she wondered "What if I had stayed after all?" Then one day she came across the hadith of Umm Zar: "My husband is Abû Zar. But who is Abû Zar? He covered me in jewels. I put on weight because of the good food he gave *me. He honored me to the point of having a good opinion of myself...*". This passage in particular reminded her of all the times Henry had belittled her to the point of breaking her. She knew that despite her hesitations in the face of the new difficulties she was encountering, despite her desire not to put her children through this separation, she couldn't go back to the slaughterhouse. She just felt like dying. So she started to live again. Little by little.

Her ex had seen her new blossoming and didn't miss a chance, a mistake or an oversight to get back at her. They had joint custody and this was painful for the young woman because it forced her to maintain a link. She had to accept that he could see her children. The youngest was very similar to her in character. He was a happy child full of energy, but as soon as he was with his father, his behavior changed radically. He no longer had the same appetite, and smiled little or not at all. But he was back to his old self as soon as he went home to his mother.

But... that was what Henry was doing. He was sucking the life energy out of them. To attack his children was in a way to attack her. She had applied for sole custody but failed. Undeterred, Solena had hired another family affairs specialist; the case was underway. And the young mother never failed to invoke Allah in her prayers. She talked a lot to her children, not to denigrate their father but to encourage them, to remind them that they were brave and that despite the harshness of the situation, she loved them more than anything. "Everything will improve insha'Allah". In the meantime, she had to put up with her ex's toxicity, her endless reproaches and insults. It seemed that she had forgotten to put the prescription in the children's bags. He called her an "unworthy, incapable, irresponsible mother"! All in the same message. "And what do I do if the little ones get sick? Have you thought about that? You really are a bad mother!" Solena knew it was an exaggeration. Knowing the 'man' who was a true Drama Queen, she had learned to get past his constant need to put her down. After the separation, with time, she had learned to stand back, but there were times when words got to her and all her new-found self- confidence went out the window. She'd snapped just after that idiot Morsam had unmatched her. Not so much because the bad behavior had hurt her but because, honestly, it was too much for one evening.

She had enjoyed her solitude after separating from her son's father. For her, it was like being released from prison. Little by little, Solena had regained her self- esteem, able to speak a sentence without having to search for hours for the right words or stutter. She had regained some color, a light on her face that was accompanied by laughter and smiles. Shopping... that had been something she'd quickly abandoned. No longer buying for pleasure. She had gone from being an ultra-coquettish girl to a shadow of her former self. Wearing clothes that were too baggy, or that didn't really suit her. And now she was taking Cynthia and Miriam shopping! She had regained a taste for reading. Oh, Allah knew how much she had enjoyed and benefited from her solitude. But after a while, once her situation became stable and her children no longer needed as much attention as when they were small. She noticed that she attracted the attention of men, and found herself enjoying it. She felt visible again, beautiful and confident. She felt the urge to share her time with a man.And that's when she started signing up for Muslim apps... She didn't know how to describe herself at first, it had been so long, it was like relearning how to introduce herself to the outside world. Besides, the men who approached her weren't serious. Disappointment. She very quickly unsubscribed. Only to sign up again on the latest app in vogue "Myhalallove. Fully aware of her qualities... but not many men want to marry a woman who is already divorced and has children. Henry had once said to her in a message: "No one wants you or will want you. You're useless!" Solena sighed. Sitting on one of the deckchairs in front of the pool, shielding her eyes from the sun with one of her hands, she looked at Cynthia who was coming towards her with a large bagpack. Today there was a little trip down to Muscat to see the city and eat in a restaurant. Just as her friend had arrived and was encouraging her to get up and join the group, the woman's phone rang. She had just received a notification. She put the phone away in her own bag. She asked: "What did you put in your bagpack to make it so big?" Cynthia looked at Solena: "Only useful things. Food, buddy."

Cynthia had told her friend that they would both have a "carefree" day. She tried not to let intrusive thoughts absorb her, but it was difficult when the tour guide turned out to be your suitor. Liam was walking a little further with his brothers. She was with a group of sisters. Scattered about or walking nearby, there were couples with their children. Fewer than on the last outing, as some had decided to make their own excursions and visit the city on their own. The young woman felt caught up in the beauty of Muscat. She was also able to appreciate the kindness of the Omani people and how welcoming and modest they were. The fact that this country had long been protected from mass tourism meant that its inhabitants had kept a certain innocence.

They made you feel welcome, naturally. When she and Solena had gone to the market, one of the women from whom they had bought abayas had invited them to come and eat at her house with her family. The girls kindly declined the offer as it seemed complicated and they didn't want to go alone. It felt so good to be welcomed but also respected. Here, people didn't look at you with hostility. And it had nothing to do with the fact that the girls wore veils because some of the travelers didn't, but they were just as respected. Cynthia could imagine herself living in this country, walking on the beach and the turquoise waters of the sea. She imagined herself with Liam. They make a stop to the Sultan Qaboos Grand Mosque. Liam held back so as not to stare at Cynthia. He really felt a joy in knowing she was there even though they weren't talking to each other. He was trying to keep a cool head. Because, man! This girl was driving him crazy. He thought of her eyes, her mouth, the way she spoke, her habit of carrying her hand to her lips when she looked at him... He wanted to spend more time with her and talk to her. He stopped the group at the entrance of the mosque. Giving instructions, where they have to meet. There were two entrances, one for women and one for men. He quietly watched Cynthia sneak inside the mosque. Then, after checking who was present and who had gone to pray, he went back to the side of the men. He used to come here, but the beauty of the place of prayer always took his breath away. And he felt so much serenity. It was the place where he liked to spend the most time. Mainly to recharge and forget the issues at work or everyday life and remember Allah. He prayed intensely, asking God to grant him Cynthia as his wife. For their side, Solena and Cynthia were also amazed at the interior of the mosque. It was the second time they came but for them it was like a new first time. The walls of the main hall are covered in white and dark grey marble panels that are decorated with geometric designs and motifs from nature. The dome which overhung them, opened on a huge gold plated chandelier. The interior was as rich and luxurious as the interior was. But above all the peace that one felt once in the prayer room was incomparable. She invoked Allah and ended her prayer by asking him to grant her Liam as her spouse and not to let any obstacles get in their way.

Chapter 14

Girl Boss

"Man does not get tired of asking good (things from Allah), but if an evil touches him, then he gives up all hope and is lost in despair" "When We show favor to someone, they turn away, acting arrogantly. And when touched with evil, they make endless prayers f'or good" [**Verse 49 and 51, surah Fussilat**]

Kassandra had fallen in love many years ago, but it had ended in failure. The man she had loved had only approached her for her money. She had met him at a time in her life when she felt fulfilled as a woman. He was working in a law firm and his dream was to open and create his own business. Kassandra, on the other hand, was succeeding professionally, working for a marketing company. She wasn't dependent on her parents or anyone else. She had a superb flat in New York and a group of girlfriends. For a long time, the young woman had been one of those who embraced her career and "didn't need men". But after years of celibacy, dating zeros she'd found on Tinder or at parties, she had finally met the man she considered her future husband. They both shared a common ambition. Gone were all her 'girl boss' and 'Alpha woman' convictions. With this man, she had allowed herself to be vulnerable. She had laid down her arms. Open to the idea of a love story. Kassandra had begun to invest in her fiancé″s project, supporting and encouraging him. Their relationship seemed solid. So she began to settle down and take the time to dream of a married life. But the happiness was short-lived. One day, she caught the man calling a woman. She played dumb, pretending not to have seen or heard anything.At the same time, she was observant. Watching her man's phone calls and messages as soon as his back was turned, after subtly stealing his password. Until the evening when she pretended to be out. In fact, she'd waited for him to go out too because he was clever, and if he was seeing anyone it certainly wasn't in their flat. As soon as he went out, she discreetly followed him by car. Unsurprisingly, she saw him passionately kissing a woman who was none other than his best friend. A real cliché. Since that day, she had given up on two things: men and supposed friends. It's hard to trust anyone again after a blow like that. So she chose to have fun and live from day to day again. Her last relationship had been with a very nice waiter, whom she had finally run away from, avoiding all his calls. She wasn't interested in the people in her circle, but the fact that she was seeing someone who didn't come from the same background didn't reassure her either in the end. She was afraid of suffering again. And she was looking for herself. Studying, working, getting married, and then growing old and dying. That was how she saw life. But wasn't there another goal? Sometimes she just felt that her life was going in circles. With no real purpose. From the outside, people might say that she had everything to be happy. But without lying, she found that only the poor told her that. Yes, she had everything, but she was no happier than anyone else. She had a good lifestyle, she didn't have to worry about how to pay her bills. If she wanted to treat herself, she didn't count her pennies either : The best places, best food, clothes. When she went into a shop, the shop assistants recognised her. Chanel, Louis Vuitton, Yves Saint Laurent, just some of the brands that filled her wardrobes and drawers. But that was where the happiness ended. Once the pleasures, whatever they were, had been satisfied, she was back where she started. She felt a great emptiness. Which she filled with other easily accessible things: sex, drugs, alcohol. Yet another cliché of the rich girl Something was missing from her life. Something bigger, something more meaningful. All her disappointments, and her existential questions led her to learn about different religions. She had tried Hinduism, but it seemed too complicated. She'd tried a religion that looked like Scientology... But no thanks. She wasn't prepared to give her fortune to the first guru she came across. Catholicism? She didn't understand the notion of the Trinity, but she'd tried hard. It wasn't really clear to her. Finally, she had given in to the positive affirmations. Being by nature rather stressed with her work, she started the morning by listening to her CD. "I am me, I am unique. Nothing can touch me. All around me are positive vibes and love. The earth is my bubble. I am my own bubble…" However, when the new girl in the department received the promotion she had been working for almost a year, the truth came out. Behind her wheel, stuck in traffic. In between assertions of "I am me" and "I am unique", she had to face the truth: One of which was a "Fuck oooooffff" followed by a succession of insults. That's when she realised that it really wasn't for her either. The CD was soon smashed and thrown in the bin. Kassandra had been fascinated by the development of her brother, with whom she was very close, and who had taken up the Islamic religion. A real hothead at one time, his life was messier than her. How had physically survived the mediocrity of his lifestyle ? And it was this that made kassandra a believer. Yes, she had witnessed her first miracle. With his new religion he had radically mellowed and seemed much more fulfilled and happy.It was an other miracle. So she said to herself: "If he's happy, why can't I be? And she started to ask him about it.

The young woman still had difficulty with was ablutions. It took her so long to put on her makeup every morning, it was almost religious. But she had made an effort because her well- being and her new religion took precedence over everything else. All the pain and the accumulated sadness had vanished. She felt lighter, more fulfilled, happier. Kassandra continued her learning by reading a few books and even the Quran in its translated version. She had also started a few Arabic lessons, but because of her work, she didn't continue. She also tried to go to the mosque on Fridays. It was incredible how welcome she felt after pronouncing her Shahada. She hadn't told anyone about her conversion Not even the girlfriends she felt closest to. They met dressed up and wearing makeup. When alcohol was served, Kassandra just said she'd stopped drinking. She was the first to down a whole bottle. This surprised those around her, but they took it as a sign of real awareness, of maturity even. And then the young woman stopped eating pork and other non-halal meats. That's when people started asking her questions. But she was inflexible. She didn't want to tell anyone. Only her brother knew. She and Liam had always had a rather cold relationship with their parents. "Money can't buy happiness". Their childhood was further proof of that. His parents weren't bad, but they'd raised them to succeed. And they were counting on them to succeed in their business. There wasn't really any room for feelings or moods. And if there was, it was muffled in gifts, a trip or a reception, expensive clothes. No room for affection or big discussions. Just the minimum. Their parents forced them to concentrate 100% on their studies. Friends? They were either an opportunity or a threat, especially if they got in the way of their success. Her mother had told her: "Always watch your back because you never know who will stab you in the back" and also "Women are the most vicious". Her mother, who had previously been a model and then a beauty queen, always boasted that she had rubbed shoulders with the dregs of the dregs. "People can be gentle as lambs with you, while their hearts are black with jealousy".

Her parents had already sabotaged the relationships she and her brother had with other people. Love, friendship, whatever. Only those deemed good enough to rise in society were allowed into their personal lives. It was a toxic, stifling climate, in which, in the end, the young woman never knew if the people around her were really there for her or out of interest. And she mistrusted everyone. Did they really laugh at her jokes? Did they really sympathize with his misfortunes? Nothing seemed authentic. Fortunately, as an adult and through her job, she had begun to make her own experiences of people. Friendships, although sometimes superficial, were initiated by her and not controlled by her parents. You could say that she and Liam had practically brought themselves up alone. Surrounded, of course, by nannies who changed regularly. Their mother Martha had never tolerated her children becoming attached to women other than herself. Growing up like that had hardened Kassandra. She didn't trust anyone and it was hard for her to get attached. Above all, she felt it was her duty to protect her brother. And at the same time, she feared losing him. Religion had definitely brought them closer together. They used to get on really well, but now they shared a common belief. However, Kassandra was having a bit of trouble finding spiritual fulfillment. It was difficult for her to give up all her habits and especially to adopt new ones, such as getting up at 5 am, praying 5 times a day, eating strictly halal food... She'd last a week and the following week she'd be in Ibiza with her gang of girlfriends, or at a restaurant eating slices of Italian ham. Her veil? She was convinced of its benefits, and although before her conversion she saw all veiled girls as submissive and soulless, today she had become their fervent defender. But as far as she was concerned... She wore it mainly to please her brother and only in his presence. She knew it was hypocritical of him. But she preferred to go gradually rather than wear it strictly and stop overnight. She felt ashamed and didn't yet assume her belief to the point of revealing it. She and her brother were a family, without their parents. They stuck together more than anything. And if she wanted to make someone proud, it was him. Allah didn't seem to answer her, she felt sad, frustrated, and unhappy. When she confided this to Liam. He replied: "Allah is with you as you think of him". Her brother... Always responding with parables, and always using symbolism. He had lost her with his philosophy. But she had more or less understood the principle. "When can I be happy too?" His brother had explained to her that in everything you had to be patient. And that trials were always followed by something better. But despite this, deep down she couldn't convince herself. She told herself that because of everything she had done, perhaps she was being punished. She didn't feel deserving of Allah's blessings and goodness. She had a secret. Something that ate her up from the inside. Kassandra hated herself . Would Allah help her to overcome this? When she read this hadeeth about the Messenger of Allah ﷺwho said, "**Allah Almighty** says: Whoever comes with a good deed will have the reward of ten like it and even more. Whoever comes with an evil deed will be recompensed for one evil deed like it or he will be forgiven. Whoever draws close to Me by the length of a hand, I will draw close to him by the length of an arm. Whoever draws close to Me the by length of an arm, I will draw close to him by the length of a fathom. Whoever comes to Me walking, I will come to him running. Whoever meets Me with enough sins to fill the earth, not associating any partners with Me, I will meet him with as much forgiveness."

The young woman knew that the answer was « yes ». Yes ! She could find redemption, yes, one day she would be able to love herself, to make peace with herself. She decided to get rid of half her designer bags and most of her many luxury clothes by selling them. The money she made from this she donated to Muslim charities. And frankly, she felt a little better. Doing good around her was like filling her heart with a sense of well-being, a feeling of finally being useful for something. Not just living for living's sake, but being the cause of someone else's happiness.

Kassandra was used to having everything at the moment. Patience was not her strong point. So she knew that change would take time for her to adapt to her new life, but it was worth it for her. She was in dire need of a "rebirth". And now, as a Muslim, she wanted to settle down again, get married, and have children. She felt ready for that. Beautiful and intelligent, men liked her but felt unable to set up boundaries. So they approached her easily. She wasn't yet comfortable with her faith and, although she didn't respond to their advances, she couldn't help wanting to seduce them or to be seduce. This abstinence and non-mixing thing was the most difficult thing for her, especially with her job being her refuge. Even if she understood the principle and was totally in agreement with it. The application was a different matter. Her parents were Catholic. When she was younger, one of her aunts decided to become a nun. The life of luxury was poisoning her, she told them. Kassandra wondered how anyone could devote their whole life to their religion, without sharing it with anyone, without physical contact, without sex. She would ask her aunt sometimes. For her, men and women were made to be each other's companions. A human being could not live alone according to her perception of things. And that was also what she had learned about Islam from reading books. This religion did not deny this aspect of life at all. And that was just as well because she had lived a full life and very active and it was absolutely out of the question for her to give up all sexuality! The day she saw Samuel arrive, she said to herself, "If Cynthia doesn't want him, why shouldn't I?"

There he was, tall and solid, dark with close cropped hair and breathtaking eyes. 100% his style. Except that her eyes were turned towards Cynthia the prude. It was from that day on that she had hated that girl. It was even worse when she realized her brother's interest in her. Cynthia...was that the only reason to hate her? No. She just didn't like her. She didn't trust her. Liam was naive. He'd always made the worst choices about women. As her sister, she didn't want to see her brother suffer or be duped for his status and money. Ah, he would do anything to distance himself from their parents. Hide how rich he was and live simply. Like driving in his eternal jeep, while he could buy any luxury car and up to 2 or 3 but he played the modest and preferred to invest in "useful" things or to help some charities. Which was ridiculous. It wasn't going to help him meet the right person. Kassandra was determined to put an end to his marriage plans. She had to get that "saintly" woman away from her brother. which to her seemed to be a charity...Several days earlier, as soon as Liam had told her of his interest in "Sainte Nitouche", she had contacted Samuel, his uncle who ran the hotel, so she had access to all the bookings. The young man had seemed surprised and then, finally, Kassandra had managed to convince him to return to Muscat to get back the woman he loved. She was now going to meet him. Not wanting to arouse the suspicions of her brother or of that parasite of Cynthia, she decided to go directly into the young man's bedroom. Samuel opened the door, not expecting to see her. He looked as if he had just come upstairs as he was changing. "Come in, but please hurry". Upon entering, she observed that the brother appeared to be well-organized. Only a suitcase on the ground was open and placed on the floor. He has taste in clothing," she said to herself. "Cynthia has just had a meeting with my brother, to get married as explained on the phone." Samuel seemed to be a confident man. He looked at her, listening attentively to what she had to say. It was hard to make out what he was thinking. "Okay, and?" "And things seem to have gone well because my brother is making plans. You told me you were in love with Cynthia and that you and she were about to get married... Do you remember why you came here?" Samuel sat down on a chair next to a table that was opposite his bedroom window. Well, not exactly; it was just a marriage proposal that didn't go through," he added with a sad smile. Then," he continued, "I don't owe you anything." Kassandra made no secret of her disappointment. "So what are you going to do?" she asked. Unlike you, I don't want to destroy those I love. I'll see if Cynthia is genuine in her feelings for him. If she does, I suggest we leave them. I have my own plan.» « Like what? Serenading her? Your proposal was quite pathetic.» « Jealous ? » He replied with a smile. Disappointed, Kassandra didn't know what to say. She hadn't expected him to give up so easily. "In her mind, she had imagined that he would fight to get Cynthia back. "I think that at the rate things are going, it's not too late to stop this farce. Samuel ran his hand through his hair, then his face, still looking at Kassandra. "I don't see what you have to gain from this. Let's be clear: I didn't come here to take part in your vendetta or to harass the girl I love. If I see I'm wasting my time, I'll just leave." His voice cracked and he lowered his head. Kassandra seized the moment to approach him. He raised his head. "You'd better go, I've got things to do." Confused, the young woman got up and left the room. She wished she were in Cynthia's shoes right now. Feeling all the love this man felt for this woman made her even more aware of her own loneliness and need for affection. By separating Cynthia from her brother, she was now convinced that it was the best thing for them.

"And she left the room, furious at having wasted her time. But she had one last option. She dialed a telephone number. A woman's voice answered at the other end of the line. "Hello?"

Cynthia had found it very difficult to sleep. Her heart was filled with sadness as she recalled the moment when Liam had ignored her. She got up and did her ablutions. Had he changed his mind? She remembered a magnificent verse: *"And whoever shows piety towards Allah, He grants him a way out and gives him sustenance from where he does not expect it; and whoever trusts in Allah, He is sufficient for him"*. This gave her the strength to invoke Allah and beg Him to allow her to make the right choice for this man for whom she had developed feelings. She finished by saying her consultation prayer: "Lord, I have come to take counsel from Your knowledge and to draw strength from Your strength. I have come to ask You for Your infinite generosity. For You are able and I am unable, You know and I do not know, and You are the Great Knower of unknown worlds. Lord, if You know that marrying Liam is a source of good for my religion, for my life here below, and for my future destiny, designate it for me, make it easier for me to fulfill it, and bless me. And if you know that marrying him is a source of harm to me for my religion, for my life here below, and for my future destiny, turn him away from me and turn me away from him. And predestine for me the good where it is to be found and inspire me with its satisfaction." Peaceful, she went back to bed. "I trust in Allah now". And she fell into a deep sleep.

The next day, after Fajr salat, she knew it was best to be transparent and honest with Liam. After all, he was the man she wanted to share her life with. She shouldn't be afraid to talk to him and be honest with him. She went down to the hotel restaurant. Solena was already seated at the table. There were croissants, local pastries, and fresh fruit juice. "Salam Alaykum, I've ordered you a hot chocolate," said Solena with her mouth full. "Wa 'alaykum salam. Thank you, are you all right?" Cynthia hadn't forgotten her mood the other night. Since then, she hadn't hesitated to check on her friend regularly. So much so that she called her little mummy and even asked her to leave her alone. "What? Is your life going to end now? Stop asking me if I'm all right!" By the grace of Allah I'm not on the verge of suicide." She was being ironic, but when she said the word suicide, even though it was ironic from her point of view, Cynthia didn't even crack a smile. "I'm doing very well Alhamdulillah". Today, a new outing was organized to see the camels. They were both looking forward to it. The other girls and families in the group were gradually arriving. Couples with children seemed to have been there since early morning. Some were getting up to leave their tables. "Look, there's Liam over there." Cynthia jumped to her feet. Running, before the astonished eyes of her friend. She hurried to catch up with the young man before he left.

"Liam, I need to talk to you." She wasted no time. She told him about Samuel, about how they had met, about their marriage plans that had come to nothing. "I came to Oman because I wanted to get away and have some time to myself, and to recharge my batteries religiously too..." And shyly she added, "And then I met you and since our exchange, you're the only one I have in mind and with whom I want to share my life. She gave him a sidelong glance, waiting for his reaction. « I've been searching for a long time and now I feel at peace with myself when I say that I feel we were made for each other. » She told him. The young man looked at her intensely. He wanted to take her in his arms and was fighting not to. « I appreciate you coming over to tell me that...Especially after that guy's performance. Seeing your...colleague declare his love for you in public did leave me a bit puzzled." "Well,I'm not that easy," Cynthia replied, smiling. "You are a great woman and I feel the same way about about you. I really want to carry on until the marriage insha Allah If it's all clear to you, then it's clear to me too ». He smiled at her, and Cynthia smiled back. In the distance, Samuel saw them. He felt jealousy tear his heart.

Chapter 15

She's Not that bad finally

"And whoever shows piety towards Allâh, H e grants him a way out and sustenance from where he does not expect it; and whoever trusts in Allâh, He is sufficient fo r him", [**surat 'AT-Talâq 'Ayah 2/3**].

Yesterday, Liam had avoided Cynthia despite himself. He didn't know how to behave with the young woman now that the man he thought was her ex-husband had returned. He'd done his best to suppress the love and attraction he felt for her, but it was hard to get it out of his head when he was working so close to her. He felt that the story was complicated but for him, it was worth it. Cynthia was worth it. Their discussion earlier had just reassured him of her feelings for him. At the same time, Kassandra arrived with her dark glasses covering her eyes. "Liam, can we talk please?" They sat down at a table. "Cynthia was never married to this man. She lied from the beginning. What I did find out was that he proposed to her." She remained silent to weigh up the effect of the words she had just said. Liam looked at her. "Okay...Thanks Kassandra. I know all about it". Cynthia told me everything. Kassandra made a gesture of annoyance. And shook her head in denial. "And you're still going to persist with her?" asked Kassandra. Liam was surprised to see so much anger in his sister towards the woman he loved. He couldn't understand it. He looked at his sister for a long moment before answering. He felt at peace that Cynthia had come to him and told him the whole truth. His confidence in her had never wavered but he had felt the need to be reassured about his feelings. And that had been the case. "Yes, I'm going to carry on with her. Just be happy for me. Accept it." Kassandra said nothing. Her brother got up and she watched him leave. Liam went to reception. Samuel was there. "Salam Alaykum, I'd like to speak to the hotel manager." Liam watched the man talking to him, and above all he wanted him to leave as soon as possible. After listening to Cynthia, he knew that there was nothing innocent about this man's presence and that he had feelings for the young woman. Worse, he was there with the sole intention of convincing her to make a life with him. He felt himself boiling. But he replied calmly: "He's not here at the moment, I'm replacing him, what's this about? Let's take a seat over there," and as he moved forward, he invited him to follow him to an isolated lounge of the restaurant. They sat down face to face in comfortable armchairs. Liam wondered what Samuel's real motives were. Why was he still here when Cynthia had turned him away? Was he going to try something again? Samuel confidently took out his MacBook Pro and placed it on the table, turning it slightly towards Liam. "I'm the representative of a major pastry company for corporate catering and large hotels. We have a whole range of pastries for you to choose from and in particular our latest creation, 'Le Cynth'. Liam couldn't believe his ears."Dude, did you seriously come to pitch me pastries? "Liam thought inwardly. He couldn't believe what he was hearing. Samuel showed a presentation photo. "It's a delicious sponge cake with a strawberry center, topped with light mascarpone cream. This cake is light on the outside and passionate on the inside", he concludes, proud of his presentation. "The Cynth...started Liam, like Cynthia?" He had settled himself at the back of the armchair, his arms resting on the armrests and his fingers digging into them. He didn't know whether to laugh or explode. "Yes, that's it, like my wife's name..." Samuel didn't have time to finish. Liam interrupted him. "What are you talking about? She's not your wife and you know it. I spoke with Cynthia. And she has no intention of marrying you, man. You're wasting your time and I think you should leave the hotel!" Samuel felt rage seize him. He watched this man, full of confidence, tell him that HE Samuel no longer had a chance with the woman he loved!? The pain was doubled because Cynthia hadn't spoken to him since their last discussion. The proposal didn't go as he had expected... but knowing Cynthia didn't surprise him. He had acted in a desperate way. He knew his cause was lost no more hope about his future with her. Still provocative he answered, "I'm also thinking of a cake called Le Kassandra, pure on the outside, a slut on the inside, what do you think?" Liam lunged at him and threw a punch, to which Samuel responded. The noise attracted a crowd of people who watched the two men fight. Waiters and other customers intervened to separate them. Kassandra and Cynthia arrived at this point, shocked by the scene they were witnessing. Liam and Samuel's faces were swollen. Samuel was dabbing at his bloody lip with a damp handkerchief he'd been given. Cynthia ran to him. "What happened? Why did you fight? Samuel looked up at her. His gaze was hard and jaded. "Forget it. Tomorrow I'm leaving. I should never have listened to that psycho Kassandra." Kassandra? What's she got to do with it?" asked Cynthia. "Samuel stood up, leaving the young woman to face her questions. Kassandra helped Liam to his feet and took him to the infirmary. And then, she proceeded to clean his slight wounds and apply ointment to his swollen eye. "What were you thinking? His brother was holding an ice pack to his eye. A waiter had given it to him. "He literally called you a slut." Kassandra burst out laughing, but her laughter was choked in her throat when Liam added: "You know him." "I just wanted to help you," Kassandra answered softly. I called him because it was clear there was something between him and Cynthia. I'm no saint, but I love you." Liam looked at her in disgust. "It's not about being a saint, you know that, but you know where we come from our past. And you're doing what our parents did, invading my privacy to control everything. Cynthia is the woman I'm going to marry insha'Allah. Whether you like it or not. And if you pull any more plans to stop me..." He didn't finish his sentence but Kassandra knew he wouldn't hesitate to distance himself. Liam straightened his head. All he could feel was pain. "Kassandra, you know I don't want to hurt you. Just focus on your own life; I don't need you protecting me. It hurts me more than anything else!" And he left. Cynthia was still reeling from what had just happened. She decided to go back and see

107

Samuel. She needed to have a chat with him. She passed Kassandra, who seemed preoccupied. The young woman's eyes were red and puffy as if she had been crying. She intercepted her and held her by the arm. The young woman pulled away abruptly. "What do you want?" Far from being put off, Cynthia replied calmly. "How is your brother? "If you really want to know, go and see him!" Cynthia started to walk, then turned around and quickly joined the young woman. This time, she wasn't going to let her go. She grabbed her by the shoulder, forcing Kassandra to stop. "May Allah help you. You really are a monster. I've never seen anything like that in my life! You treat people like shit," Cynthia continued angrily: "You're ruining everything by behaving like a mediocre person when with a little effort you can be a great person. Your brother...he's a wonderful person macha Allah. It doesn't matter if I marry him or not. What matters is that he's surrounded by loving people who he can count on. But now I'm wondering who you are for him ! "O- M-G, it looks like everyone's made a date to come down on me...So far I've mostly seen you ruin his life." Replied Kassandra "Samuel told me you were involved in this. So you're the reason they're fighting!" answered back Cynthia. "Oh, I don't care what your ex said. Since you've been in our lives, we've had nothing but problems". But Cynthia didn't let her guard down and continued: "I don't think I'm the problem here. You've got a nice hijab, but to claim to be Muslim, that's not enough. I think having the attitude wouldn't be bad either." And she looked the young woman straight in the eye. Kassandra smiled fiercely at her, her eyes misty with tears. "Who do you think you are? You think you're better than me?" "I'm no better than you." Replied Cynthia. When she touched her arm, Kassandra pulled away violently. Cynthia continued talking. "I assure you, I'm not perfect either. You've seen that.But that's no reason not to encourage each other to be good, " she concluded. "I just don't let you walk all over me and that's what pisses you off. You can't stand it. Nor can you stand it when I tell you the truth." Liam's sister smiled again, but this time she had softened.

"You've got a temper. You'll be a pain in the ass for Liam." "Probably, but as long as he's surrounded by people who mean him well...That's the main thing."

"Yes," admitted Kassandra. And the young woman put her sunglasses back on. "By the way... my brother must be outside in his car... He likes to take refuge in it when he gets depressed... She added sarcastically and left her to walk with her regal gait. Cynthia saw Liam's jeep outside the hotel. She knocked on the tinted window. Liam got out of the car. His face was badly bruised and his beautiful black hair was a bit disheveled, but it added a bit of a bad-boy edge to his good-boy style. "Salam alaykum. How are things? he said, trying to look relaxed. "Your sister told me I'd find you here. Cynthia smiled to see him so embarrassed by the situation. She would never have believed that a man like him could go off the rails. He seemed so in control. "Yes. I'm sorry you had to see that...I don't usually explode like that...I humiliated myself a bit in front of the customers..."Cynthia smiled at him and wanted to say something, but he interrupted her. "Cynthia, think carefully about the decision you're about to make. Your ex is here for a reason. Besides, what is he to you?" "Nothing. He is nothing for me. Like I said, he wants to marry me. But it is done, it's past history." As she said these words, the young woman was confident in herself. "He's not the man for you anyway. » "Because you are?"

Liam replied immediately, "You know you deserve better, and yes, I think I'm someone for you." He got out of his car.

"I'm suck at cooking and baking...But I can make pancakes." Cynthia chuckled. « I don't feel I'm competing with this guy at all. Not when I'm sure that I'll give you everything you need. » This time he was looking straight at her. She felt her heart beat faster. All the feelings she had for this man were rising to the surface. "I want to marry you. I've never changed my mind about that. I don't want to. And nothing my sister says to me will change that. I trust you." He added, looking at her intently. The attraction between them was such that it was difficult for

Cynthia to keep a clear head. "Stop talking and marry me!" she wanted to shout at him. "I'm just falling in love. Even if it's a bit early to say. But anyway, that's how I feel. Listen, I want to do things right and not mess things up.

We don't have to wait any longer, insha'Allah. Cynthia took out her mobile, "Call my dad if you mean it. Honestly, I don't want to waste any time either. But I want proof that you're serious about me." "Okay. I'll do it insha Allah" Cynthia gave her father's phone number. Liam quickly tapped on the touch screen and registered it. Cynthia left, feeling groggy and her heart in turmoil. She was on cloud nine. He had told her how he felt... And he had agreed to call her father. She remembered her discussion with Miriam. She wanted to do things properly and by the Islam rules insha'Allah. There was nothing better than encouraging a suitor to meet the family because that was a decisive test. "You'll see if the guy's really serious about it. If he refuses, it's because he's not genuine or because he has things to hide". Cynthia was convinced of that. And she felt that Liam would keep his word and call her father. The young man was right, it was perhaps a little early to be talking about love. But one thing was certain: they were meant for each other. Then she thought back to Samuel. He made fun of her. Allying himself with Kassandra... She was discovering who he really was. Despite his lack of religious practice, she thought he at least had sense of morality and respect for her. It was shocking that he could have been up to something with Kassandra. She needed to talk to him. She was happy to have had the courage to walk away from Samuel

and grateful to have been able to meet Liam. Allah had preserved her, she was now convinced. As she made her way to the terrace, she saw Solena waving at her. As she walked towards her. he heard her name being called: "Cynthia! Samuel joined her. "Can we talk?" "Yes. I think it's the right time." Inside she was fuming at having let herself be taken in. She remembered that famous evening when she was so torn between him and Liam. Oh yes, she really had been stupid. Cynthia saw, however, that Samuel seemed ashamed and sorry about the situation. "You know, I think our cakes, especially "the Cynth", would have been a big hit here in Oman," he replied, smiling painfully with his swollen lip. "How do you know Kassandra?" asked Cynthia, cold and ignoring completely what Samuel had just said. "She contacted me. She wanted to get you away from her brother." "And so you came to her rescue?" Cynthia felt overwhelmed by what she had just heard. "I'm sorry, but in the end, I'm not really is. You threw me out like a piece of shit, you made a date with another guy, behind my back, without telling me anything. You can't blame me for coming here to try my luck and then act like you've got nothing to reproach yourself for!" The young woman felt sad for him. She now understood that he had just been used by Kassandra. "You didn't believe in us, you gave me hope, you play with my feelings and here I am like an idiot here in Oman." At these words, Cynthia couldn't help but laugh. It really was the joke of the year. Did he have an inflated ego? She thought back to all those little signs she'd seen from him when she didn't know him... to the first time he'd shown up at the door of her hotel room. I love you and I don't see what's so funny." Cynthia looked at him."No, you don't love me. You just like the idea of winning a challenge. "You like that I resist you, that I'm supposedly unattainable." She said. She knew she had hit a nerve because he didn't even try to contradict her. "I'm sorry things didn't work out between us. I'm not happy that you're sad, but the truth is we're not on the same page. I've got really expectations of life together and you're not going to be able to deliver." Samuel tried to put on a brave face. "I apologize for the last time. And it's true that I may not be the best person to marry you at the moment... I'm sorry I'm not." Cynthia felt relieved that he was admitting the truth to herself. "At least I tried. I'll never forget you. I wish you lots of happiness. You deserve it Cynthia." "And so are you. She told him. « And I'm sure you'll also find what you're looking for insha'Allah." Samuel smiled. "Is there really no chance between you and me? You know...I think I know why you chose him over me. He's got more money, a hotel manager, a big car... Obviously, despite my Apollon body, I couldn't compete". "You don't give up". "No, that's true. I'll never forget you,that's for sure. Thank you for that life lesson. Women...you're all the same!" "Well, I'm off, salam," replied Cynthia in response to his reproaches. He was really in denial. Forgetting that she'd given him an opportunity and he'd blown it. She walked away. She regretted not having made things clear before leaving for Oman. It would have made things less painful for everyone. She saw Samuel running back towards her. "Can I have the ring back, please? I'm not rich, so..." At these words, Cynthia smiled: "I'll give it back to you right away, insha'Allah. And she walked quickly away. "Okay...Cycy, think about the two of us anyway" ! Cynthia rolled her eyes at the young man. For her, everything that had happened was inevitably linked to the consultation prayer she had made earlier. She saw this series of events as a response from Allah. Events had happened so quickly. Like a rash. It had happened suddenly and surprisingly. Once he was alone, Samuel went to the beach. He really needed to think about his future. He had wasted time, he thought. But he felt relieved in fact. It had been torture to think so much about Cynthia, to put so much effort just to have her attention. In the end, she had helped him move on. Only the sound of the waves broke the silence of the night. The sky was empty of stars. The beach was lit by the lights coming from the hotels. He took a selfie and posted on Instagram. #Aloneagain. He saw a veiled woman walking in front of him. She was wearing a long kimono and a hijab. Suddenly she stopped and looked straight ahead. "You're a night owl too?" chuckled Samuel, interrupting her thoughts. The young woman turned to him: "Oh, it's you? Your new look suits you! You look like you've been beaten up by a boxer..." and she smiles. "Kassandra... Last time I didn't have time to see how sharp your tongue was." "And me how cowardly and ridiculous you were. Anyway, I apologize for manipulating you into coming here and for everything else." Samuel looked out over the waves. "I also apologize... For calling you a slut. I think you must be a good person. You've just...suffered too much and you wanted to protect your brother." He faced her. Finally she was pretty, not like Cynthia but still... »Maybe we can take a din... »Kassandra interrupted him. "I'm not into leftovers. For a man who proclaimed his love a little earlier, I think it sucks. And I made some good resolutions, I've decided to change, so... " He smiles: " Me too but you can't blame a broken man for seeking happiness elsewhere" The young woman rolled her eyes and grimaced a smile back. "Okaay Nice talk. However, I'd like to continue my walk alone. There's been too much emotion today and I haven't had my fill of dermo fillers and Botox. I can feel the weight of my worries". Samuel frowned, shaking his head. "Okay, good luck" "Thank you, salam and farewell." Samuel just looked at her with a smile that seemed to say: "Man, what a bitch..This is my day", and then silently he went his own way. Kassandra stayed on the beach for a while. If the situation had been different, she wouldn't have hesitated to ask him to get to know her. But there was no question of starting a project with a man in love with another woman. No, when it came to men, Kassandra told herself that she had to make better choices... And then... Everything that had happened and her conversation with her brother had turned her upside own. She really needed to think things over, get a grip on herself, and concentrate on her faith. She finally understood that her happiness did not lie in the hands of a man. It lay in knowing herself better. She had always been afraid of ending up alone and had finally persuaded herself that only male company could bring her the happiness and fulfillment she so desperately sought. But how could she be happy and fulfilled if she didn't question her actions? The young woman returned to the hotel. She had to start by admitting she was wrong...and apologizing. Cynthia was chatting to Solena when she heard a knock on her door. She was surprised to see Kassandra, sunglasses screwed on her nose, and her Louis Vuitton suitcases. "I wanted to apologize for everything that's happened and pass on the Salam. Can we talk alone?" Solena gave her a long look from the back of the room. Kassandra said to her, "I also apologize for the last time. I'm not... let's just say I'm not very sociable." And...Which makes you rude?" Solena added. "You could say that. But it's not a valid reason so, sorry" "Apology accepted", Solena said with a big smile. Cynthia also smiled at her, which surprised the young woman, knowing how badly she had behaved towards her. The two women left the room. The corridor was quiet. "I appreciate you coming to me," Cynthia said softly. Kassandra took off her glasses" Yes, you know, my brother and I have come a long way. I have a habit of judging and pushing people away, often without giving them a chance to get to know each other. After weeks together, I can tell you're a good person, you just talk too much...Kassandra paused as if to stop herself from saying too much. "...But you are a person we can trust macha Allah." Cynthia couldn't help but hug her. She felt the young woman tensed slightly, then slowly relaxed. Hesitant at first, she finally hugged back the woman who was to become her future sister-in-law. "I'm not leaving forever, I'll come and torment you sometimes when you marry my brother insha Allah." Cynthia gave a tight smile, not knowing whether to laugh or cry. Although her eyes were hidden, Kassandra's emotion was visible in her voice. "See you soon insha'Allah. Cynthia replied. And they split up. Solena was waiting for her, sitting quietly on her bed, starting to pack. "Honestly Cycy, I'm really happy for you that you've found your other half. But that girl...wow, she's going to be your sister-in- law. I hope you don't have a hard time of it." The two girls burst out laughing. "No, I think it's going to be fine insha'Allah. They were nearing the end of the trip and so much had happened in so little time. Both of them were in no hurry to return to France and resume their daily lives. Cynthia was finally taking a breather. She was already imagining her life with Liam. "May Allah bless you, your marriage, bless you, and unite you in happiness, little brother. Liam was busy with plans for the next tourist outing. His sister's voice disconcerted him. "Listen, Lili," she knew that her brother hated the nickname she gave him He thought it was too feminine, but it was her way of showing her affection. With her hand, she brushed aside his future protests. "I haven't got much time, my taxi will be here soon insha'Allah." She faced him and took off her glasses, revealing eyes reddened by emotion. "I wanted to thank you for always giving me good advice...even though you had a near-death experience, I don't know if you remember sometimes that I'm your eldest." Liam laughed. "Just a few minutes," he replied. "Cynthia seems to be a good girl after all. She has a good heart. Also, it would be a crime if you didn't marry her." She patted her brother on the head and took him in her arms. "I'm going to miss you, I'll call you when I get there insha'Allah". "Where are you off to?" his brother asked. At these words, Kassandra pulled out the handle of her wheeled suitcase and set off on her way. "I'm going home" Liam watched her pass through the glass doors of the hotel and into a taxi. He was going to miss his sister, but at least he wasn't worried anymore. When his sister thanked him for his advice, he knew it was because she had really questioned herself. Later, Liam got ready in his room. He knew that Cynthia liked him, he should have felt confident, but for the first time, he didn't know what to expect. He felt less confident in himself. He had put on a long tunic over trousers and combed his hair and beard while thinking about his sister's words. Why wait? He was going to propose this evening. He had prepared everything. He got off early, before the Maghrib prayer. He was feeling stressed. Later that evening, as he was leaving the hotel hall, he saw Cynthia. She was chatting to her friends but his attention was focused solely on her. She was so beautiful and radiant. Her only smile put him K.O. And he had only one desire: to make her his wife as soon as possible and to end his frustration of not being able to have her with him and to touch her... People wonder why we like this person or that person.

He couldn't explain exactly how he had come to be so attached. And he didn't feel the need to answer that question. He had been with many girls. Feelings of love were not something new to him. What was new was that now it was combined with a feeling of peace, of serenity. It was also the fact that he wanted to start a family with this person. When she was alone, he joined her: "I have something to show you insha'Allah". They went outside, the hotel, where there was a luxurious garden, with beautiful trees and a pathway lined with flowers and plants, each more beautiful than the last, and decorated with garlands of light.

Chapter 16

Marry Me

"Souls are soldiers in groups; those who know each other live in harmony, those who ignore each other dwell in discord." [**Sahih of Bukhari**]

"It is he who created you all from one man, from whom he drew his wife that he might find serenity with her."

[7- 189 Al Araf Surah]

Cynthia stepped forward, amazed by the lights illuminating the garden path. Rose petals on each side. "This is just a foretaste of what awaits you when you become my wife insha'Allah," says Liam, motioning for Cynthia to come forward. "I've had some difficult times in my life and for several years I'd given up on sharing it with anyone. I know you have a life in France, but I can offer you so much more here... He turned to Cynthia, who was moved: "I hit a man because he had given your first name to a pastry" They both laughed. "Yes, I admit, it wasn't very clever, and what's more you didn't even taste it, I've been working on it," said Cynthia with a smile. Liam put on a false air of seriousness. "Ah, I should have punched less, then." Then, with a solemn air: "I'd like to talk to you and spend time with you in halal conditions...Would you agree to become my wife?" Cynthia was torn between laughter and tears. "YES! Yes I do!" Her dream was finally coming true. She had waited so long for him to propose! » "But first I have to tell my parents and you'll have to meet them insha'Allah. Don't worry, I've called your dad, the meeting's already been arranged and I'm always a hit with the mums..." added the young man, puffing out his chest. Seeing the falsely questioning look on the young woman's face, he added: "But this is the first marriage proposal... Okay, okay masha Allah. say no more," replied Cynthia, amused. "I'll walk you back to the hotel...We'll have plenty of time when we're married insha Allah." They walked side by side to the hotel reception, burning with the desire to hold hands, hug each other and not to leave each others anymore...

But they were both determined to wait until the official. Both wanted the barakah of Allah. They parted. Galvanized by his new-found happiness, Liam smiled as he thought about Cynthia's answer. He was planning an intimate Walima with just their closest family and friends. With the parental model he'd grown up with, marriage had never been something he'd dreamed of, or been interested in. It was a project he intended to realize only if he found the one he fell in love with. And so far that had never happened. Before, he didn't mind spending time in charming company. But when he got attached, it turned out that it was never the right person. It was only when he converted to Islam that he radically changed his way of life: prayer was his refuge, which soothed him. And giving two hundred percent to his work at the hotel and as a tourist guide kept him busy. Making women and marriage something totally secondary. His love at first sight for Cynthia had taken him by surprise. The first time he'd seen her in her puma boots with big satin bows, he'd found her totally offbeat and touching... He smiled, surprisingly, this evening he'd expected not a yes but rather a "Wait, I'll think about it". She was the perfect combination of kindness and gentleness, with a great deal of self-confidence. And he liked that all the more. Up until now, he had been afraid that his marriage plans would fall through, but in the end, Samuel seemed to be out of the running... Was he really, anyway?... He doubted it. Cynthia was too good for that clown! His phone began to ring, interrupting his thoughts. "Hello?" It was her father on the line. "It's me, we're coming tomorrow to see you and discuss some things. Hannah will be there. "Okay, see you tomorrow." Liam hung up, suddenly discouraged. Finally, it was going to be more complicated than he had expected. The next day, Liam gave up his shift to his colleague. As his parents were coming today, he would not be doing any sightseeing or excursions outside Muscat. He had changed into a light-colored suit and shoes to pair with. He was nervous about seeing his parents. The meeting had been arranged at the airport. Liam had spotted Cynthia with the rest of the women from the first tourist group, and their trip was almost over. They waved quickly. No time to chat. But that was just as well. If she had known what was going on, she would probably have been heartbroken. He was tense. He would have to talk to her sooner or later. So far, everything had been going swimmingly. But his parents had decided to pay him a surprise visit... He wouldn't have been surprised if his sister had told them the news. It was only when he got there that Liam tried to regain his usual self- confidence. This was no time to flinch. He had driven to the airport. On a private runway, a plane belonging to no company landed in the distance. The stairs slowly unfolded. The first person to step out of the plane was an elderly woman, very elegant in her fur jacket. Underneath she was wearing a tailored dress. Her ash-blond hair was pulled back into a bun and she was wearing large Dior glasses. A tall man in a suit preceded her. Apart from his steel-blue eyes, Liam was the spitting image of him. The reunion with Liam was brief and solemn. Suddenly he saw his mother turn towards the plane, seemingly waiting for someone. Then a young woman appeared. It was Hannah. Her ebony black hair was cut into a plunging bob. Her almost perfect body was moulded in a white dress and she was also wearing a black fur jacket. Perched on her heels, she walked down the steps as if she were on the red carpet. Her beautiful eyes, adorned with long lashes, stared at Liam, who was concentrating on his parents. She walked straight towards him. "I'm glad to see you're not wearing the cassock, the beard is much sexier... "She whispered. And she smiled provocatively. Liam remained unmoved. He hugged his mother briefly and she kissed him on the cheek. "Mum, dad...did you have a good trip?" Cynthia spent the afternoon in the company of her friends. The association had taken them to Muscat's market one last time, where everyone had enjoyed a walk in the town and stopped to eat in one of the restaurants. Solena insisted on doing a Facetime with Miriam who wanted to get a glimpse of Muscat. This time Cynthia had bought some lovely souvenirs. Her sister had insisted that she bring back an abaya, and her mother wanted incense. The women here used incense to perfume themselves. The guide had explained that, according to tradition, they burned it and scattered the smoke under their clothes. This kept them perfumed all day long. Cynthia had literally fallen in love with this beautiful country and its people. The idea of doing the hijra here and living alongside Liam in this little piece of Paradise appealed to her more and more. Her heart was finally at peace. She felt confident. Her dream was just around the corner. Marriage had never been her ultimate goal in life. But like every human being, she needed someone to be by her side. Honestly, it was a miracle at her age that she hadn't had a boyfriend. When she was younger, although she was a dreamer, she had never been that interested in boys. As she got older, issues at home, and her father's illness, all these things led her to take on responsibilities and have priorities. All this, plus a job in a pastry shop and university, had meant that she hadn't been able to settle down and have as much fun as her girlfriends. At 24, she felt the need to find meaning in her life, especially when everything was going wrong. And that's what led her to Islam. In the end, it seemed normal to turn to marriage. She felt ready. Settled down, she was starting to earn a living, and felt serene spiritually and in her current life, but more than that... she felt the need to share it with someone.

"No obedience to a creature in disobedience to the Creator" [**reported by At-Tirmîdhiyy**].

Once they were settled at home, Liam talked to his parents about a variety of subjects. A chef had prepared a meal for them. And they were all seated at the table. The atmosphere seemed relaxed but he knew full well that another, more serious subject would be raised that evening. Hannah was not present. After the dinner, he and his father gathered in the villa's spacious living room. "Dad, I need to talk to you." The young man settled into the cream leather sofa. "I've met a girl here and I want to marry her insha'Allah. This sentence was difficult to get out of his throat. His father sat behind a solid ebony desk. "Your sister told me. She called us a few days ago." Liam felt his anger at Kassandra surge up again. But this feeling vanished very quickly because whether his parents found out now or later, it made absolutely no difference to the situation: they already had plans for him and his future. His father was as tall as he was, a charismatic and elegant man. He was a confident and self-made man who had been working since he was very young. He leaned back against his leather seat. His father inspired respect and power. "You know, when I was your age, I had some crazy dreams too...in a little while you're going to have "to run the show", as they

say. Hannah is the only woman you need to focus on...and you've known her since you were a kid." Looking his son straight in the eye, he continued: "Your childishness, your so- called religion...It's gone on long enough. You will marry Hannah. It's not up for discussion." Liam stood up, wanting to end the discussion and leave. He faced his father, who stood up to approach him. He placed his hands firmly on the young man's shoulders "Her parents own shares in our properties and companies and they have a significant fortune. If we join our both families we will be unstoppable. Plus, she's a girl from a good family and seems attached to you." "I don't like her. It's never going to work between us." "Love... It comes and goes," continued his father. "...but it's always fleeting. Your mother and I have learned to build our relationship as a couple and so will you. Love, son, isn't everything. This young woman you think you're in love with, she's not from your background, she doesn't know the codes of our world. She'll never feel at home and that will end up affecting your relationship. Believe me, it's not worth it." It was a cynical, closed-minded way of looking at life. Liam had often seen his mother cry and their parent argued when he was younger. And he knew for a fact that his father had not been very loyal to his mother. But he refrained from saying anything. He heard himself answer him: "I think differently. I am no longer the young man who came to you, irresponsible and miserable. I can run the family business now and make us more prosperous than we are now. Please...meet her. It costs you absolutely nothing." "So, let's say I accept, and then what? I'm getting old and you're my only son. Our lineage, our fortune must endure... Do you understand? You must give up this girl. You have more important things ahead of you, son. "Why don't you ask Kassandra to help you run the business? She's got a PhD in economics, she knows finance really well." "Kassandra...Well, Kassandra" said his father in a condescending tone, "She ...still has a lot to learn and acquire... Mainly maturity.She is not ready yet." He straightened up. "Don't disappoint me." And he left Liam completely bewildered. The young man was torn between the desire to please Allah by marrying Cynthia, the woman he loved. And the desire to please his parents. He was indebted to his father for giving him a second chance. Indeed, before his conversion to Islam, he considered himself a loser. He alternated between good days when he was fully conscious and helped his father run his businesses, and other days when he was completely unhinged, spending his time in bad company and running away from the family circle. In the end, he even gave up his father's business altogether. But following his conversion, finally settled and at peace with himself, he asked his father to give him another shot. From an early age, Liam had grown up admiring him, always seeking his satisfaction, affection, and attention. His father saw the good in him. He sent him here to Oman to manage their hotel with his uncle. His uncle was away, so Liam appreciated even more the fact that his father trusted him again. But it didn't come without a price. And he understood that. He stood up, facing the bay overlooking the sea. Tormented by his thoughts, he did not see Hannah enter. She slipped behind him. "You don't seem happy to see me," she murmured. Our parents promised us to each other. You know that. You had other plans, but I only had you in mind. The two of us are going to get together just like in the good old days!" She laughed. Liam turned to her. "Tell

122

your parents you don't want to marry me. We don't have to pretend."
"Who's pretending? Not me. And why? Because of your new religion?
What about your promise?" Hannah asked him. "Your promise never
to abandon me? You never loved me?" "That promise...You were going
wrong, we were so young. I loved you but not the way you think,
Hannah, it wouldn't be right for me to marry you. I love someone else.
I'd rather not delude you." Hannah shook her pretty head in denial.
"Our parents need our alliance. Neither you nor I can back out. You
risk losing everything and so do I. And I don't want to be disinherited. I
like my way of life so far" Liam left the room, he was suffocating. It was
probably a situation he would have accepted if...he hadn't met Cynthia.
And yes, arranged marriages, contrary to the clichés, did happen a lot
in posh circles. Preserving lineage, wealth, status... That evening, he
returned to the hotel to find Cynthia reading in the reception room.
When she saw him, she smiled. But when she saw his somber
expression, her smile vanished. "There's been a change. We're not going
to be able to get married. I've got business to do before, insha'Allah."
Cynthia stood up, disconcerted by what she heard. She looked at him
with wide eyes, trying to understand why her dream was collapsing.
She thought better of it. "For what reason? Can you tell me why...?"
Liam explained his relationship with Hannah, their marriage arranged
by their parents, the duty he owed to his father, his responsibilities, and
his heritage.

"Are you going to marry her?" "No, I want to spend my life by your
side insha'Allah." "Then keep your promise to me. Tell them no." "It's
not that simple," Liam continued. "I feel like such a loser right now.
I'd like to understand. I'd like to understand why you're giving up your
happiness for money?" Added Cynthia, her voice breaking. Shocked
that the man she admired and could see herself married to was prepared
to enter into an arranged marriage. "Nothing is definite. I don't intend
to marry Hannah. But I need to buy some time... To prove to my
father that we can do without this marriage". They looked at each other

for a long moment. Cynthia was overwhelmed. She could feel him slipping away and there was nothing she could do about it. Kassandra had been right: she knew nothing about their world or the codes that governed it. In the distance, Hannah appeared and walked towards them. She gave Cynthia a curious look. Scanning her from head to toe. "Your father is waiting for us." She murmured to Liam. Cynthia was stunned. Here was her rival - the equal of a more natural and younger Kim Kardashian, but sexier. But wasn't the situation bizarre? If not totally illicit? And Liam was going to tolerate this? What kind of nonsense was this? Of course, he was. How could she compete with a woman like that? She thought, taking her eyes off the beautiful stranger. "Do what you want Liam. Thanks for the chat". And without looking at him, Cynthia left as quickly as possible so that they wouldn't see her crying. She stopped in the swimming pool outside, recovering the belongings she had left on the lounge chair, and stuffing her book into her handbag. Then, once inside the hotel, she rushed to her room. There had been too much misunderstanding for one evening. The next morning Cynthia packed her bags, her heart heavy and her head full of questions. Although her heart was set on this country, she was so devastated that it was a relief to return home. Especially at such a painful time. The organized holiday was over.

Unlike the driveway, the departure was filled with bitterness. Liam had come, knocking on the door to let her in. But she didn't. He apologized. But for the young woman, it was over. A page had been turned. She had to turn over a new page. Because if she didn't, she wouldn't have the strength to hold back her anger and her tears and move forward. She had cried all night and prayed so much. Solena was as overwhelmed as she was. Would she ever get over her broken heart? Solena had tried to console her as best she could, but had resigned herself to seeing her friend cry all night in her bed. When Cynthia opened the door that morning, she saw a folded piece of paper, which someone had probably tried to slip under the door. It was her 'husband project' list, with a note at the bottom. "I want to marry you, give me some time to sort it all out, I love you". She then had a flashback to the moment when she had stopped to put her things away. The sheet must have slipped and Liam had fallen on it. She reread her the words she wrote down, tears welling up in her eyes. "You matched all the criteria, but waiting for you...?" she mused. As she went downstairs with her luggage, she saw Liam with a tall man with whom he had the same family resemblance. A classy woman with grey and long hair an the sexy girl who was with Liam the day before. She looking at Liam. He was as elegant as the day before, wearing a dark suit, a shirt without a tie and loafers. His face was closed and his gaze sad. She wanted to take refuge in his firm arms. Instead, she fought hard not to cry. Their eyes met one last time. Time seemed to stand still. Cynthia was the first to look away, her heart heavy. Maybe one day they would see each other again. She had a good time that she would never forget...

For the moment, it was a door that was closing.

Chapter 17

Liam

And the example of those who donate their wealth, seeking Allah's pleasure and believing the reward is certain,[1] is that of a garden on a fertile hill: when heavy rain falls, it yields up twice its normal produce. If no heavy rain falls, a drizzle is sufficient. And Allah is All-Seeing of what you do.

(Surah Al Baqarah, verse 265)

Later that night, Liam had just got up to go for a swim. On his way to the terrace he found a small piece of paper with a handwritten list. He didn't know Cynthia's handwriting but he knew it was hers...

If she knew how much he loved and desired her, he'd found much more in her than just criteria to tick off. She made him feel complete. But now it was too late to turn back. He had to keep his promise to his father. It wasn't about money, no. It wasn't about inheritance either. He was earning a good living, had saved and owned property and investments. He could build his own legacy. But he could never buy his father's trust and repay him for everything he had done for him when he was at his worst and had dropped out of the family business. According to Kassandra, it wasn't about love but about control and manipulation. But for Liam it didn't matter, it had saved him from himself.

He split the turquoise water of the pool one last time, swimming at full speed in an impeccable crawl. His warmed- up muscles stood out from the effort. He got out of the water and picked up his towel.

He knew that even exhausted by his swim, he wouldn't be able to fall asleep and stop thinking about Cynthia. Knowing she was sad had been a blow to his morale... It was worse knowing he was at fault.

He went back up to one of the hotel rooms where he was sleeping, which was reserved for staff only. After a long shower, he changed into comfortable clothes and reread Cynthia's note. He added a few words that he hoped would comfort the young woman and made his way to her room. He slipped the folded paper under the door. The temptation to knock and persuade her to open the door had been too strong.

The next day, he got up to make his salat and stayed awake to lift some weights and do abs workout. When he could, he ran around the hotel or along the long, often empty road that ran alongside the beach. But not this morning. He had to prepare the welcome for the new arrivals, leave instructions as he would be away, and make sure everything was ready for his uncle's return. A meeting was scheduled for later in the morning with business partners. But what motivated him most of all was the hope of catching a glimpse of Cynthia before she left.

Later, he joined his family and Hannah. Later they were due to take a private jet to Dubai. He had never felt at home in this city subhanAllah. It was so superficial, with a cruel lack of soul. This was also one of the reasons why he decided to move to Muscat in the Sultanate of Oman. It's a city full of authenticity and history, faithful to its past although gradually opening up to tourism. Families could be seen strolling around, even into the evening. People could invite you into their homes to share a good meal without even knowing you. Mountains, palm trees and date palms surrounded them. The town centre had been modernised without destroying the old houses and buildings. The market rubbed shoulders with the malls. It had become his home, alhamdulillah.

Surrounded by his family, he saw Cynthia and was immediately drawn to join her. Their eyes met. He had so much to say, he couldn't take his eyes off hers, but in the end it was she who looked away first. He watched her walk away. Liam's heart was torn. He had wanted to follow her but knew that it would have made things even more difficult. From a distance, he could hear his parents and his uncle talking, and then Hannah's voice making mocking remarks: "Is she one of your groupies? You're always such a hit, I see".

"Liam, I see you've managed the hotel well in my absence, can you show me the books? It was his uncle who brought him back to reality.

During the car journey to the small airport, his father shared with him a file that was a summary of a future acquisition. So much had changed since they last met with Hannah. Before and especially since his conversion to Islam. "How many customers are we meeting today? Liam looked at her, "We have the Level Company and Mr Lee, a businessman who wants a contract for seaside hotels." With perfectly manicured hands, Hannah took the file from his hands. He had said all this without looking up at her. Without looking directly at her. He could see that she was offended.

He wanted to keep some distance between them... And not give her any false hope. Not only did she make no secret of the fact that she still had feelings for him, but now that they were promised to each other by their parents, she was doing everything she could to get his attention and take advantage of her almost 'fiancée' status, and all with the approval of her father and mother. The next day, Liam's mother organised a meal at their flat hotel. Hannah's parents were there this time.

The young woman was dressed in a white dress with floral prints, flat shoes and light make-up. They were all seated at the table, where the food was expertly presented, each looking more delicious than the last. Liam's father stood up to make a toast. "Yesterday we closed 2 contracts worth 1 million dollars, and I'd like to congratulate my son on the way he's pulled it all off," Liam smiled modestly. His father continued, "You know we've known Lucas and Elise for years, and to see our 2 children united by marriage is also an achievement. Celebrating the wedding this summer seems like a good idea" Liam knew that far from being a simple idea, it was an indirect order. His father wanted him to ask for Hannah's hand in marriage and organise their union. The whole family at the table raised their glasses in celebration of the new lovebirds. Hannah turned to Liam with a smile on her face.

"Have you thought about the date of the ceremony? She told him later, as they helped clear the table.

"Hannah..."

"I've already chosen my dress and tomorrow is the fitting day...I want you to be there."

The young woman's parents interrupted them. Hannah's mother resembled her daughter; she was just as brunette and had the same penetrating gaze, but although her face was marked by expression lines, it was clear that in her day she had been a true beauty. Her brown eyes were highlighted by a skilfully drawn line of kohl. She wore elegant glasses and exuded calm. She was also very elegant. When he was young, Liam remembered all the afternoons spent in their big house in Ireland. The hot chocolates in the warmth of the fireplace and how she sometimes acted as a second mother when Liam fled his parents' house to avoid their arguments. It was during this period that he and Hannah had grown closer. That time when you start to see your parents' flaws and realise that they're not perfect. The need to confide in someone, the serenity of knowing they were being listened to... And then, barely a month later, Hannah had become his first girlfriend. It hadn't lasted, but the young woman hadn't forgotten or put up with the fact that he had ended their relationship.

Her father was very tall and rather thin, so there was a family resemblance with Hannah, but that was where it ended. He was a somewhat self-effacing man who spoke very little but was surprisingly close to his daughter and didn't hesitate to shower her with gifts when she asked him to. "Tomorrow

Liam, Hannah is going for fittings, will you please go with her?" Hannah's mum looked at him over the top of her glasses. Yes, he would go with her even though he knew it was a mistake. However, it was also an opportunity to set things straight...

The next day, the young man left the hotel where their family had rented flats for their stay. Dubai, a modern city, dominated by towering skyscrapers, where anything was possible and where tourists, influencers, entrepreneurs and investors were storming the streets in the early hours of the morning... The sun flooded the streets, the sky a heavenly blue promising high temperatures. He was wearing a dark green polo shirt and knee-length trousers. He crossed the street. A driver was waiting for him and opened the door of a luxury car with tinted windows. He sat inside, enjoying the air conditioning after the stifling heat outside.

Hannah was waiting for him in a designer wedding dress boutique called 'Yours'.

Inside, luxurious wedding dresses were displayed and hung preciously on golden hangers. Further on was a department for the ladies-in-waiting, although they were more modest, the silky fabrics and the details in the stitching still inspired refinement and splendour. Hannah arrived with her body moulded in a long gown of lace and pearls. The strapless dress revealed the beginning of her chest, and the long train was attached to her hair, which was styled in a bun. She smiled brightly at him, her lips shining and her cheeks slightly rosy. "I've been waiting for you for at least an hour!"

"Sorry, I had a few phone calls to make. The young woman lifted the train that was preventing her from moving, helped by the sales assistant. "Thank you. Can you give us a few moments? »

When they were alone, Hannah hesitantly approached Liam. "How do I look?" she said, her eyes slightly misty. "You are beautiful... And the man who will marry you will certainly be the luckiest"

"Liam... It's our turn. You're the lucky man who will make me the happiest woman in the world. She continued, standing before him, her eyes now weeping, "To see you always with other girls than me... All these years waiting for you... I love you." She couldn't help but touch her arm.

«We already talked about this wedding and you know very well what my thoughts are about it» murmured Liam.

"You talked. I only listened to what you had to say out of kindness." She looked at him intensely through her long black eyelashes. The disappointment on her face. "Liam...these marriages are what our families have been doing for generations. But you and I are lucky, we're not bad..." She continued with a smile on her lips "And we love each other." She says all this as she approaches the young man, her eyes always fixed on him.

Liam was facing her with all his height. "I love another one. And you know I'm never forced to do something against my will."

"Ouch," Hannah said as if she had just been punched. "You mean the little groupie from last time?"

«It is not a groupie, it is the woman whom I will marry insha Allah.»

"You will not go against our parents' orders. You have no right to do this to me! Think what we will lose if we do not unite!" Anger and sadness devastated her beautiful face. "I never forgot you. How could I?" She raised her hand to caress Liam's face as he stepped back. «You are the only one for me and you will always be,» she added in a whisper.

"Hannah, things have changed since we were 17. And I would still hate to break your heart but... I'm not worth putting your life on hold for me. You have to move on. And as far as inheritance is concerned, I will do everything I can to ensure that we do not fall..."

This time, Hannah let tears flow. "I don't care about that money if I can't share it with you. I would never know why we're not together and it frustrates me. What do others have that I don't have?" She let go with a desperate look.

He knew the answer...When they ended up dating, Hannah had become obsessive, jealous pervasive, Oh man! Although having access to her cell phone, social media, and password, she was still suspicious, she couldn't stand to see him talking to other girls than herself as part of ongoing work, asking for a pair of shoes in stores... it was almost crazy. Many came to him to denounce the threats and other attempts at intimidation that his girl used to prevent them from approaching him, talking to him or even daring to breathe in his face. Hannah was... dangerous. As for their relationship... She was systematically worried about not satisfying him. He had to review her outfits, her choice of place for dating... He was thinking, it was necessarily that he had a reproach to make to her or that he thought of another... But of course, he had broken up, man! He was patient, tried to protect her from people, and tried to open her eyes to her own behavior. But it always turned against him.... The last nail on the coffin she was a daddy's girl. Who had this constant need to be reassured, who had luxury tastes and a sharp love for the material all this added to an irrepressible need to control it... From 17 years old! He had just felt suffocated and had quickly regretted that things had become intimate. Did she change as an adult? Of course not! He knew it, saw it, felt it in his gut. His beautiful angelic face, his demented body, his skin that seemed soft and smooth... All this was bait for the most naive. He was no longer fooled.

"I would say what you have, that they don't have Hannah. They don't have my unconditional friendship. And that cannot be replaced just by love. You are unique. You are like a sister to me," he added with a fatherly air. The young woman looked at him questioning. His tears had dried. "You will never be like a brother to me. Never!" She said without shouting, but in a tone as sharp as a knife. Eyes again fogged.

Liam put back his sunglasses.

"I sent a file to our lawyers, and here is a copy. It is important that you read it knowing that we will now work together insha Allah. There will not be a wedding just so that things are clear. We are and will only be business partners. If you have any suggestions, let me know." Hannah was now completely destabilized.

"You're a bastard!" she exclaimed, "Here's my suggestion, why don't you take your file and go fuck yourself?" And she joined the gesture with the word, aggressively raising two fingers with long and manicured nails.

"How lovely. Have a good day, Hannah," Liam replied in a sweet tone as he walked out of the store.

When Hannah angrily removed her veil, and her train, the saleswoman who earlier helped her for her fittings, appeared out of nowhere, alert, to retrieve them.

Liam inwardly thanked Allah for allowing him to take a different path than his parents had prepared for him. He could never stand the fury and the spoiled child side of Hannah. Islam had really opened his eyes to his life, his expectations for himself and the people around him.

He quickly returned to his hotel for a shower and put on a jogging suit and t-shirt. Earlier in the morning, he and his lawyers had discussed a new contract that would bind him to Hannah but also established rules regarding its implications in family matters. He wanted to protect himself from everything that would be haram, he would have a right of view on the customers with whom he would work, would come to galas and other receptions only for a limited time in the duration, no late business parties in places where women and alcohol met. He knew that many clients wanted to sign their contracts in places of debauchery with everything that involved, sex, alcohol, drugs... It was kind of part of the game. Behind the scenes of the business world and powerful people.

But Liam wanted to have the satisfaction of Allah and make clean money at all levels even regarding partners and customers...

Suddenly, he felt the need to find Cynthia. Rediscover its sweetness, simplicity, authenticity and their discussions... He had a year to put his project of success into execution insha Allah to show his father that he was ready to take up the torch when needed. But would Cynthia wait for him and marry him after all this time?

Chapter 18

Hard Reality Hits

On their return to France at the airport, Cynthia and the group of sisters immediately returned to what they had left behind: the prevailing Islamophobia. The sidelong glances because of their hijab or the way they were dressed. Oman already seemed like a dream. "Thank you for your interest in our company. We regret to inform you that we will not be taking any further action on your application" Before going up to her studio flat, Cynthia retrieved her mail from her letterbox. As she climbed the stairs to the building, she felt her heart racing. Anxious just at the thought of reading the mail. She opened the blinds and curtains that kept the rooms in darkness and moved into her living room. The companies she applied to all turned her down. She knew the refusal phrases by heart. And that didn't even surprise her, because as soon as she walked through the door for an interview, she knew when she left whether she'd been rejected or not would be taken or not. And for her to be accepted, she had to remove her veil. "Her parents regularly gave her this advice. "Take it off, it's only for work" No thanks. That was enough sacrifice. She had unpacked her suitcases, put half her clothes in the washing machine and the other half, still clean and folded, straight into her wardrobe. The young woman badly needed to relax. She headed for the shower and as she opened it, the nozzle of the shower hose fell, hitting her foot. She screamed in pain. There was also a leak from the hose. She had plugged it up with some kind of putty but apparently, it was all going live... She finished showering, collecting the water directly into her hands. Checking her bank account, Cynthia saw that she had exactly 200 euros left to see her through to the end of the month. 15 euros would go towards her mobile phone subscription and 25 euros towards her Internet subscription. Maybe 30 or 40 to replace the shower head and hose, plus shopping for food... The rent had already been paid Alhamdoulillah. Reality hit her hard. She had done her calculations before leaving on holiday, but she hadn't foreseen that she would have a problem with her shower. It would be good if she could find a job insha'Allah. There was no question of relying on his parents. They already had too much to deal with themselves. She thought about meeting Miriam at the grocery shop. It was exactly 12 o'clock. Maybe the two of them could go to a local snack bar and get a burger.

She was really feeling down. But she was looking forward to seeing her friend, who had not been told when she would be back. When the young woman went into the shop, she saw Miriam in deep discussion with a handsome young black man. He was athletic and had a devastating smile. He and Miriam were holding hands over the checkout counter. When she saw Cynthia, Miriam was startled and quickly let go of the boy's hand. Both became embarrassed and the young man quickly left. "What happened there?" Cynthia asked, shocked by the scene but especially to see that her friend was secretive and not just any. Miriam, came out from behind the register. "Cynthia, I have too much to tell you..." The two girls were sitting face to face. Miriam told everything from the beginning, how she had known Ousmane, her desire to marry him but the fear that parents judge her for having hidden all this and oppose marriage because of its origins... Cynthia wiped her mouth, as she had just eaten her sandwich. She was too hungry. She swallowed and said, "Girl, I'm not going to hide the fact that I'm so disappointed that you kept all this from us. I'm your friend, and so is Solena. We support each other. That's who we are. It offends me that you didn't trust me enough to tell me about Ousmane." Miriam looked full of guilt. "It wasn't a lack of trust. It was a shame. Everyone sees me as the good girl, the one on whom you rest, who does everything right... And lately, I have advised you and Sol' not 209

to see men alone... And there... I am myself in this situation. This is really not the kind of thing I thought I could do!" « That's exactly what friends are for. They are there to help!» Cynthia said in a reassuring tone. "I am not here to judge you, but to advise you. And no one is perfect. You know that Samuel came to see me in Oman?" Miriam widened her eyes with astonishment. "NOOON! Don't tell me there was drama?" «There was» Cynthia told her briefly how the young man had proposed to her, and then fought with Liam" "And what about Liam?" «Tell me first what you are going to do about Ousmane» replied Cynthia dipping his fries in mayonnaise. «And then... You will not be seeing each other in there until the end of time... » With these words, Miriam burst into laughter. "It was the only way to keep things halal!" «Darling, there is nothing halal to see a man who is not your husband, with whom you flirt, with whom you caress the fingers...» Cynthia continued in a slightly sarcastic tone. «I don't caress them!» Miriam said embarrassed. Cynthia smiles. "Nah, but you know what I mean. Today you're holding hands, tomorrow what? It can't last. I came in and I immediately saw and felt how attracted you were to each other. You are a couple...And you go well together masha Allah. You must marry." Cynthia took another bite of her burger and when she swallowed, she continued: "I know you're ashamed, but you have to tell your parents. Besides, you don't think anyone sees you, but I remind you there are surveillance cameras all over your grocery store. Do you really want your parents or your cousin to find out your little secret before you talk about it?" "Ousmane wants to meet my parents, but I'm the one who postpones every time." Miriam, drank a few sips of orange juice. «I will talk to my parents tonight incha Allah» "Yes, go for it...Can I have your fries?" The next day, Cynthia took the metro. It was packed. She thought of Liam, who had abandoned their wedding plans to save his inheritance. Just thinking about it... Solena interrupted her thoughts. They were both sitting on the train to Châtelet-les-Halles. A woman sat opposite them, staring at them with an air of contempt. The girls chose to ignore her. And continued their discussion. Miriam needed their help to choose her wedding dress. "I know you're sad, but don't let it get you down. Allah will give you the right job when you least expect it. Solena continued with emphasis "as Will Smith says in The Search for Happiness: If you have a dream, you have to protect it. Those who can't will tell you that you can't. If you want something, fight for it, full stop." With a disabused look on her face, Cynthia side eye Solena. Then she replied with a touch of irony: "You know I'm not going to watch that film again, don't you? Solena raised her arms in resignation.

The next few days were difficult for Cynthia. She felt her heart being torn apart. And she found herself in a kind of lethargy that would never end. She just didn't want to do anything else. She thought about Liam morning and night, remembering the scene where he told her they weren't going to get married. She also remembered the good times, like when he had confessed his feelings to her. She smiled then. Her moods oscillated between profound sadness and sometimes bordering on depression. Miriam and Solena both did their best to help her through her distress. Giving her reminders, forcing her to get out of his studio to get some fresh air. And that worked for her, but as soon as she was alone with herself, it all started again. She felt numb most of the time. Not so much because of Liam, but because she felt disappointed in herself. She'd gone on holiday hoping to forget her disappointment in the steps she'd taken to get married. And now she felt frustrated at having let herself fall in love with someone for whom it wasn't reciprocated! Frustrated at remembering his face, his smile, all the qualities that had led her to let her feelings flow. Loving under these conditions hurts. That was the worst part. How could she have been so stupid? Anyway... She looked up and there was a crowd in the shop where Cynthia and her friends were. Today Miriam wanted to do some shopping in a popular area of Paris to find THE wedding outfit. This was where all the restaurants, dress shops, jewellers and Indian grocery shops were. She had already been to quite a few shops. And had decided that this would be the last. Afterward, the girls planned to go to a restaurant. As they say: "After the effort, the comfort". Miriam had taken her courage in both hands on the very day of her discussion with Cynthia.

When she got home her parents were in the kitchen. Her mother was cooking. With fear in her stomach, Miriam began by saying «I love someone and I want to marry him» Her parents had both been caught off guard. But Miriam had continued by telling in what conditions, she had met Ousmane. How she appreciated the fact that he did not miss never the Friday prayer at the mosque. How kind and well educated and practicing he was, she evoked the fact that he was an ambitious young man and as she shared the will to become a doctor.

How they encouraged each other in their study... She knew that they had found her a suitor from their country and especially from the same village. But she wanted to marry Ousmane and no one else! She said something about it.

"Your father and I prefer that you marry someone of your origin because sharing the same culture will make things easier, but if it's your choice... We support you." How much the young woman had felt relieved of a weight!

Her father had explained to her that before they would not have thought like that but that they wanted to see her happy and that if this man was a practitioner, that was all that mattered to them. Ousmane had come the next day. Miriam's mother had immediately appreciated him. For his father on the other hand it had taken more time because he was not racist but the fact of seeing some young people in the neighborhood often find themselves in conflicts, and preferred to deal instead of going to school, he had ended up developing bias. But little by little while talking with Ousmane he saw that the young man was different. He appreciated his intelligence. And they even had things in common regarding entrepreneurship and finance. Ousmane had officially proposed the hand of their daughter, then they had decided on a wedding date.

"What do you think of this one?" Miriam emerged from the narrow fitting room. She was dressed in a long, beautiful traditional dark purple outfit that was covered in beads and embroidery. There was a long veil called a shawl in the same color as the dress which she had placed over the top of her head.Solena and Cynthia were amazed.

"You're beautiful Allahumma barik, you look like a princess straight out of Bollywood." Miriam smiled at them and posed. "Do you like it?" Cynthia was moved. She was looking at her friend whom she had known since their middle school days. They had shared and grown together. The shy teenager with acne was now a bright, beautiful young woman about to get married.

"Even if it didn't work out for me, I'm so happy to see that you're going to take the plunge masha Allah. » "Stop it, Cycy, you're going to make me cry", and Miriam wiped her eyes. Solena offered to take a selfie of the three of them. Next week, their friend would be a married woman insha'Allah.

The shop assistant took Solena and Cynthia's measurements while Miriam completed her purchase with some jewelry. On their way out, the girls were so hungry that they wasted no time looking for a restaurant.

It was easy in the street they were walking along, it was all there was! At the end of the day, Cynthia was back home. Her belly was full. They had stopped off at an Indo- Pakistani restaurant where they were served full plates. The girls had to take the rest to go. They got their money's worth. Before parting, the three friends had stopped off at a prayer room located between Ménilmontant and Couronnes, another area where they used to go to buy religious books. When they said goodbye, it was already the end of the day. Cynthia went home and put the bag of food she brings from the restaurant on the little table in her kitchen.

She had had such a good day that Liam had finally got out of her head. But now she was missing him again. She prayed, showered, and was about to go to bed when her phone rang. It was Miriam.

"Salam aleykum Baarak Allahu feeki for coming with me today " Cynthia laughed. "Well that's normal, we weren't going to leave you for such an important moment. Your dress is so beautiful Masha Allah." They chatted for a while about everything and then Miriam suddenly took a serious tone. "I sensed that you were really down today, even though you were smiling, you seemed clearly out of it." "I know you miss Liam but you've got to pull yourself together" Cynthia agreed: "There's that but you know there's also the fact that I can't find work. I've got a degree, I've got skills, and companies only see my veil" Miriam took her up on it:

"It's true, sister, it's not easy, but you're not the only one. Look at me I'm stuck at the grocery store for the moment, I'm not going to complain it's true... Well forget it I'm not the best example. But you can imagine that there are other sisters who are having just as hard a time. And don't worry, I'm going to recommend you to my father, insha'Allah. And if it doesn't work out, don't be discouraged. As my mother says, perseverance is our true friend! Cynthia smiled: "That's true." On the other side of the phone, Miriam continued: "And also...Before you met Liam, you had a goal and that's what you have to hold on insha'Allah. Remember that everything will come when Allah wants it to. I know it's not easy to hear. Especially when we are on trial. But there is a hadith which says that the strong believer is better and more loved by Allah than the weak believer...". And Miriam recited in Arabic, then in French the rest of the hadith: "Seek energetically all that is good for you, ask Allah for help and never weaken. If misfortune befalls you, do not say: "If I had done such and such a thing, he wouldn't have done it to me. But say: "Allah has foreordained it and what He has willed, He has done", because the word if, opens the way to the work of the devil." How these words soothed Cynthia's heart.

Even though she knew all this, she had really needed to hear it, to be reminded of it. "So dry your tears because next week I'm going to need the whole lot of you!" Cynthia smiled on the other side of the phone. It was true that in her sadness, she had neglected everyone, including her friend who was soon to be married and had needed his support in the preparations. "You're a great girl. You don't need anyone to tell you that to believe it, pull yourself together". And it was with these valuable discussions that Cynthia later fell asleep with a light heart. The next day, the young woman showered and went downstairs to collect her mail. On her way back upstairs, she came across a smiling Madame Bakri. "Come to the house for coffee or tea. I've baked some biscuits" Cynthia had already been to her old neighbour's house. Once before. When she had just moved in. To see this gentle, kind-hearted little woman, she didn't have the heart to refuse his invitation. She was a woman of North African origin who had lived in the building for years. 30 years to be exact. Her children, now grown up and married, lived in Paris or other French cities. But they continued to visit her every weekend. During the week, the old woman visited her friends, did her shopping... Cynthia didn't know her husband, or at least she'd never met him.Not being particularly busy, Cynthia accepted this new invitation. She really liked Madame Bakri's flat. The living room was decorated in a modern style. The only thing that reminded her of her origins was a Moroccan sofa that ran the length of one wall, cream-colored with arabesques, and impeccable. In the middle, there was a large oriental carpet on which stood a round woody table. At the far end of the room was a modern chest of six drawers with a Quran on it. Cynthia took off her shoes at the entrance and sat down on the sofa. Madame Bakri wasted no time in bringing her tea and the little cakes that Cynthia had loved since she first tasted them. "You don't seem to be in very good shape lately". "Nah I'm good Alhamdulillah. Thanks." The young woman didn't want to say too much because, although the lady was nice, Cynthia didn't really know her. Madame Bakri seemed to sense this because she did not insist. "You see Mr. LeFourge? He's my second husband." She said with a slight accent. As Cynthia stuffed the biscuits into her mouth one by one, she listened attentively to the old lady. "My first husband was a good, hard-working man, and we had 5 children. When he died, I found myself all alone. In this country, with no one around me. All my family is in my origin country. I had to bring up my little ones on my own. Allah gave me the strength. Later, when they grew up, I found myself alone again. For years. And I'm going to tell you something, my child." She served Cynthia again, who was still listening with her mouth full of cookies. "Never live for a man! If you don't have, you don't have. But don't stop living because a man didn't give you the attention you needed." My husband was good, masha Allah. May Allah have mercy on him, ameen. But he had his faults. After his death I had to wait a long time before to find someone else." "Later, Allah gave me another husband. Alhamdulillah. He's no better or worse than the other one. But I'm grateful to Allah because he came at the right time. During my time alone, I spent more time at the mosque, I learned Arabic and I made the hajj with my brother who returned to live in Morocco, then she leaned over and said "Who's going to blame him? Have you seen the state of this country?" As she spoke, she filled Cynthia's plate with freshly baked biscuits. "In short, today I'm happier than ever. Because I've got my children, I've got a husband, I'm happy. But the most important I have is Allah. If you concentrate on him, he will never disappoint. You can't rely on creatures but you can rely always on the Creator." Then they talked about everything and nothing. About how you could hear the whole neighborhood because the walls were too thin. It was Madame Bakri who noticed that. Cynthia got up and thanked the lady. As she was leaving, the lady said to her: "Don't worry about Liam, he'll be back insha Allah. Cynthia was shocked and was about to reply, but the old lady had already closed the door. "She hears all my conversations!" She realized, stunned and at the same time amused by her neighbor's audacity. Although grateful for her advice, she thought she should be more careful when calling people...Especially her friends.

Later, Cynthia sat down at her computer. She had to find a job. She reworked her CV and sent it to dozens of companies: working in a shop, cleaning in a hotel or office, working in the kitchen or in a call center. She was broadening her horizons. Even if the companies she was interested in had turned her down, today was a new day. And she gave her all to her research. Bills have to be paid at the end of the month. She no longer had time to feel sorry for herself. The holidays were over. All those discussions she'd had with her friends had brought her back to reality. A reality that she was once again ready to face, with Allah's permission. Looking back, she thought about everything that had happened to her. All her trials had been difficult, but that was what had strengthened her. No regrets. Allah knew exactly how to plan things and each step had been a preparation for something bigger. Knowing Samuel had greatly strengthened her faith. She was about to succumb to his advances and take the easy way out just for a bit of fun and company, but she had refused, which led her to Liam, who was everything she wanted in a man. But he had rejected her for fear of losing his inheritance or whatever. Which finally brought her back to herself. Remembering that nothing comes easily in this Dunya. As believers, we will always be tested in our faith. And it was precisely these last few years that she had felt week a profound decline in his faith. All accompanied by sadness and despair in the face of difficulties. It's at times like these, when you don't know what to do and you think you've hit rock bottom, that your faith is tested the most. Some will resort to drugs, alcohol, sex, or simply abandon prayer, their belief because they no longer believe that Allah is going to save them. We believe that he has abandoned us, that he doesn't hear our calls or doesn't want to answer them. Cynthia remembered how much she had enjoyed learning the sura Ad-Duha because, in the explanations, it is said that revelation ceased for a time, which plunged the Prophet (ﷺ)into deep distress and sadness. He feared that he had committed some fault that would have led to the anger of his Lord and his abandonment. And Allah revealed to him this surah which consoled him by telling him that the Revelation had not been interrupted because of a displeasure on the part of Allah, but that it had been necessary. Nothing was done by chance. Madame Bakri was right. Cynthia would come out stronger.

If she didn't get married now, it was just that Allah wanted her to accomplish more things or to be ready when the time came. And as for the work, she was learning patience and trust in Allah. And when the time came, she would find insha'Allah. Her life wasn't over. That was just the beginning.

Chapter 19

Allah always has a better plan for us

Anas ibn Malik (may Allah be pleased with him) relates that the Prophet (ﷺ)said: "The greatness of the reward is proportional to the greatness of the test. And when Allah, Exalted be He, loves a group of people, He tests them. Whoever, therefore, is satisfied [with

Allah's decree] will have the satisfaction of Allah in return and whoever is dissatisfied with it will suffer the wrath of Allah. »

[Reported by Ibn Majah]

"We welcome the new rising star of the patisserie world" Cynthia felt the heat rush through her and her stomach was in knots. In front of her was a crowd of people. The lights and the flashbulbs were making her feel hot and all she wanted to do was go home, take off her scarf and everything else, and relax in a bubble bath. A middle-aged woman handed her a trophy, which Cynthia accepted with great joy and emotion. "Thank you." Seeing that her interviews were going nowhere. She had often been turned down by companies. Despite her diplomas and qualifications. "Thank you for coming, but we don't accept the veil..." So she threw herself wholeheartedly into another, more specialized course that would enable her to work on her own in any country. She had just taken a break for her friend Miriam's wedding. The girls had had such

an emotional time on this important day. She couldn't miss it. Then she returned to her project, more focused and determined than ever. To finance her studies, she entered a competition in Paris. After so much hard work, today was the moment of consecration. She had won first prize, which consisted of a scholarship, a work placement in a famous Paris pâtisserie, and a KitchenAid Artisan mixer. So her joy was at its peak. "Thank you for selecting me...". Her parents, her sisters, and her friends Solena and Miriam were in the audience, cheering her wildly. As Cynthia faced the crowd from the podium and waved, she recognized a familiar face. She felt herself fainting and her heart was beating wildly. "I would like to thank my parents, my sister, and ... He looked at her intensely and smiled from his beautiful smile who melt her heart. His calmness contrasted with the rest of the people around him. "And my friends for their support". She wanted to get off the stage and run towards him. But when she remembered the reason for their separation, she made a huge effort to concentrate on her speech. He didn't applaud her, but you could see pride and affection in his eyes. Why was Liam here? A wave of hope began to grow in Cynthia's heart She didn't know if she'd have the strength to avoid him, but she was ready to hear what he had to say... If not, what explanation could she give for her presence here in France?"

Her father was doing much better, his illness seemed to be coming to an end, which was a joy for the whole family. He was sitting on the sofa in the living room, reading his newspaper. His mother was busy in the kitchen. "How are you, my daughter?" The young woman helped her mother set the table. Over the course of the year, they had seen her depressed, going through all emotional states. Liam missing her. When she was not immersed in her classes or pastry, his memory came back to her like a slap. And knowing he was promised to the pretty woman she had seen did not help her get better. She had allowed herself to love him so much, she had become so attached to him that all remained was the pain of separation. The healing had therefore been gradual. Through salah, seeing and talking to her friends, her big sister and finally have plans and goals in her life, all this helped her to get back on track. And most of all she remembered Liam's promise to come back to her. But although she still trusted him, and especially after seeing him the last time, she did not want that thin hope to grow in her heart and let herself be guided by it. Today she was just in peace and had finally accepted the situation. And even the idea that she maybe would never see Liam again... Her cheerful father made no secret of his pride in Cynthia. "I'm fine, Dad. I've got some customers for pastries this week, so I'm really happy!" "I'm not worried about you, you're very intelligent and resourceful; you'll end up taking off! I've got former colleagues who'd be interested in placing orders" "Incha Allah" added her daughter with a big smile.With the award of her prize, Cynthia had been approached by well-known restaurants and patisseries in Paris. Much to her parents' dismay, she decided to turn down the offers. She was not prepared to give up her veil again and delay her salat. She could work at any place, any country her goal was to open a business in a Muslim country insha Allah. It was her practice and her faith that had enabled her to recover so far from her trials. There was no question of making sacrifices just to succeed. Her prize had restored her self-confidence and self- esteem and she decided to set up her own business. She had transformed her tiny kitchen area into a pastry workshop. Sometimes she went to her parents' house, where the kitchen was bigger and had more work surfaces. She had invested in equipment and found suppliers like Metro, which was the best known and for which she had a card that gave her access to discounts. Miriam had helped her to get business cards. She made personalized pastries on demand. Thanks to social networks and word of mouth, Cynthia was beginning to build up a small network of customers. Eventually, her parents had come to see the benefits of her entrepreneurship and now they were her biggest supporters. The whole building and neighborhood knew about Cynthia's business. In fact, the neighbors of their building didn't hesitate to go out of their way ring their doorbell and take their order. Even though her parents said they wouldn't be disturbed, for their peace of mind, Cynthia had set up a timetable and a telephone number and email address, encouraging people to contact them before coming. Her parents weren't Muslims and although they didn't agree in every way with her new lifestyle at the time, they tried to support and understand her as best they could. It was difficult for her mother at first because she felt abandoned. But by sending her daughter to settle down, not that Cynthia was particularly agitated, but she had noticed a positive change in her. Before, Cynthia was rather withdrawn, and not very open to the world. Always worried and anxious. Focusing on her father. Once in Islam, it was as if a weight was lifted from her shoulders and she accepted that she couldn't control everything. But that only God was in charge of everything. So she began studying pastry-making and gave it her all. She was happier and more serene. And it was a pure joy for her mother to see her daughter finally be fulfilled. She had never wanted her children to carry a burden on their shoulders. Concerned about their father's money and health. Despite his illness, Cynthia's father had always been a hard worker and, with his wife, they had managed to maintain a decent standard of living. Their daughters would lack nothing and wouldn't have to worry about them until they had made a life for themselves. The young woman's mother looked at her with pride and love. "Cynthia, please set an extra place. Your sister will be here in an hour.""Ah, but I didn't know!" "Yes, it was decided at the last minute, you know with her pregnancy she's pretty tired. His younger sister replied sarcastically: "but what motivates her is if we make her favourite dish … " They laughed. They all sat down at the table, in good spirits, chatting about everything and anything. Suddenly, in the silence that had just fallen, her father spoke up: "Cynthia, we're proud of you for everything you've achieved. We didn't always understand your decisions, but now we can see the fruits of them. Your mother, your sisters, and I love you. And I also think that you have other people around you who love you, real friends, and that reassures me because if I have to leave this earth, I'll know that you're not alone… " Cynthia saw her father struggling not to let his tears fall. She stood up and hugged him. "O Allah guide my family. May have mercy for my parents just as they had mercy on me when they raised me as a child", she thought. Her heart overflowed with love for them. "Dad, why are you saying this now as if you were going to leave? They were interrupted by the bell ringing at the entrance. Her mother stood up, "I believe you have an order". They watched her walk to the door to open it. Her father wiped away his tears and took his daughter's hands, surprised by the emotion she saw in him. He never usually showed himself so troubled. In fact, he was the kind of man who never let his feelings show. "I'm not the one who's going to leave at the moment, at least not until your mother has decided on a destination... "To which Cynthia and her mother laughed. And he added, his eyes once again misty behind his glasses, "and he added, 'It's you." And when the young woman looked up from her father, she saw Liam enter the living room. He was looking at her, smiling. He was so handsome and she had missed him so much. She couldn't believe he was there. She was about to say something, but too stunned to speak, it was he who spoke first: "I contacted your parents again to officially ask for your hand for marriage." "...If of course you still want me?" he added indecisively. All Cynthia wanted to do was jump into his arms. But she held back. And laughed, too moved, overwhelmed by emotion: "I've waited a whole year! Yes, I do! Of course, I want to marry you! You've made me wait a long time!!!" Her little sister retorted, "FINALLY!"

Cynthia was wearing a long white satin abaya and matching hijab. She wore a crown of white and pale pink flowers and had her nails done. Her friends were dressed in pastels and nudes. And they all had henna done on their hands by one of Madame Bakri's daughters. Even Cynthia's sisters and her mother, who was very moved, had agreed to play along. On the other side of a huge curtain that divided the wedding hall in two. Accompanied by two brothers to represent him and an imam, Liam was dressed in a Qamis that made him look like a Prince.

His beard and hair were perfectly styled. He looked confident and happy. Liam's parents had made the trip. His mother was with Cynthia and her family. It had been a very hard year for the young man. But he had kept his promise to Cynthia. He had worked very hard to prove to his father that they didn't need to impose an arranged marriage on him to keep the family business afloat. Hannah had not been thrilled.

But although her dearest wish was to be with Liam, her love for money was even stronger. They had reached an agreement that included several contracts and investments in foreign countries. They would be linked as financial partners. The young woman had everything to gain, in the end. This was a great advantage for her and her family.

However, Liam had insisted that they would systematically go through their lawyers and advisers to manage their affairs. No need to meet in any way. This had lasted a year. Liam had intended to discuss his marriage plans with Cynthia one more time in earnest, but his father brought it up before him. Indeed, when he saw that his son was involved and serious about the family business, he agreed to let him take Cynthia as his wife. He had announced this to her in a subtle way, as they were both returning from a business trip to New York. "When are we going to meet this lovely Cynthia? Taken aback, Liam had merely smiled. He didn't waste another minute and called the parents of the woman he loved. "I want to marry your daughter..." Today, he couldn't believe that his dream was about to come true. And even if he stood up straight, it was to avoid giving in to the stress. He saw his father talking to Cynthia's father, a world apart but what united them was this special day. Their children's wedding. The tables were elegantly decorated, but without going overboard. Liam's mother had insisted on being in charge of the wedding decorations. He was the first child to get married too, and she was determined to make her contribution. Cynthia had agreed. This woman seemed very cold at first because of her aristocratic appearance and her very posh way of speaking. But as she chatted with her, Cynthia realized that she was a kind and caring person. She also spoke impeccable French. At the end of the room, Kassandra appeared through the main door. She was dressed in a long nude dress with a matching hijab. Well aware of the As a "bridesmaid" she had been careful to wear the same colors as her future sister- in-law's friends. Cynthia was delighted to see her and ran to her side. "Woow! Cynthia, you're soo beautiful masha Allah"

"BaarakAllahoufiki my sister". "You know…I was too rude with you. I missed you honestly and…Welcome in your family!" She hugged her. Suddenly, someone asked for silence. All you could hear were a few children. The imam was heard to say: "Then he pronounced the tashahhud (the attestation of faith). Cynthia and Liam both agreed that there didn't have to be an imam. But they wanted to benefit from his reminders for themselves and their guests. They pronounced their marriage contract orally, both committing themselves to each other and promising to respect, listen to, and support each other and to educate their children in the religion insha Allah. Then he continued: "To Allah belong greetings, prayers, and all good things; May Allah's peace, mercy, and blessings be upon you ô Prophet, and may peace be upon us, and upon the pious servants of Allah! I testify that there is no god but Allah and I testify that Muhammad is His servant and His Messenger." Cynthia felt shivers run down her spine. She was moved, and at the same time, she couldn't believe that it was her wedding that was being celebrated. When she remembered that she was going to marry Liam, it was as if she had woken up from a dream again. The imam continued the speech preceding the wedding with a few verses from the Quran. She was then led by her mother and mother-in-law before the imam, Liam was present with his two witnesses. Behind them, still separated by the veil, were their guests. Cynthia had covered her face with a Niqab. In front of her, Liam was moved. But when he spoke, he looked her straight in the eye: "I promised to live with you and take care of you as your husband. I am so grateful to Allah for blessing me with a woman like you. You are now part of my universe, may Allah allow me to be a good husband for you." Drowned in her eyes, looking at him with the same intensity, Cynthia expressed herself with great emotion. She did not know if her make-up would survive at that moment. She took it upon herself and spoke in a clear voice: " I'm committed to living with you Liam, sharing your life, and caring for you as your wife. I asked Allah that no obstacles stand in our way

151

and I know today that I was right to never lose hope. And... I love you."
She was she so happy to marry him, Cynthia asked for a honeymoon
in Oman, where they had met, as her Mahr (dowry). But Liam gave
her a small dark blue velvet box containing a magnificent gold bracelet
with their initials in Arabic. With this gift, he wanted to show his
affection and love for her. Following this, the imam pronounced the
invocations of use: "May Allah grant you His blessings, may He shower
them on you, and may He unite you for the better". He was preceded
by the witnesses. The room was full of emotion, the men congratulated
Liam. While Cynthia returned to her mother, to her friends and family.
Solena couldn't hold back her tears, her makeup was ruined; she smiled
at her friend: "That was so moving!" "Mummy, Mummy, why are you
crying?" It was her daughter It was his daughter calling out to her.
Solena said to her: "Because today Auntie Cynthia is getting married
Masha Allah! Her mother and then her sisters hugged her. Her mother
was overwhelmed by emotion. Cynthia took off her niqab and hugged
her friends and family. The women would come up to the bride to
congratulate her and give her blessings. Along with members of
Miriam's family and Madame Bakri's sons and their friends, Liam had
arranged for the neighboring mosques to also be provided with the
wedding meal. They were treated to chicken, mutton, and rice dishes,
salad, cakes, and drinks. And all kind of dishes cooked according to
Omani tradition, Erythree and popular Irish desserts. He and his new
wife wanted everyone to enjoy it, as required by their religion. They
also made sure that there was no food waste. With Cynthia, they had
contacted Muslim associations and local charities for the homeless.
Still-warm dishes in trays were distributed to families in need. The
operation was huge but very well organized, and with Allah's
permission, it was a success. In the marriage hall, people were eating.
Anasheeds could be heard. When it was time for prayer, those praying
performed their salat in a specially equipped rooms with carpets. One
area for men and another for women. Miriam and Solena took their

friend in their arms. "We'll miss you but we'll see you soon insha Allah."
The day was coming to an end. With their hearts pounding, Liam and
Cynthia met again at the entrance to the wedding hall. They could now
stand side by side, holding hands. They were both moved. Liam bit
his lip, then said, "I love you my wife" and placed a kiss on her lips.
The young woman just closed her eyes to feel their sweetness; it was
her first kiss. He took her face in his hands and kissed her forehead.
"I love you, my husband" she replied with a heart full of love. Then
he hugged her. "What energy !" Cynthia laughed. "Sorry, I've waited
so long for this moment, I can hardly contain my joy". The young
woman did not want to spend her wedding night in a hotel or in her
studio. She wanted to go back to Oman. And despite the hour-long
flight, Liam agreed to his young wife's crazy request. He had prepared
everything. They changed in the changing rooms of the wedding hall
and after thanking and saying goodbye to everyone, they left for the
airport. An 8-hour flight. They were already very tired, but they were
together, hugging and holding hands. Exchanging sweet kisses. They
were married for the sake of Allah. The first day they arrived, they
went straight to the house where Cynthia and Kassandra had met. They
shared the same bed, but Liam didn't want to put any pressure on his
wife. She was finally by his side and it made him so happy. « Now that
you're mine, it's torture to wait, but I can be patient. » He said, kissing
the inside of her hand. Cynthia lay down on the bed against Liam. She
removed her hijab, revealing her curly hair. It was the first time Liam
had seen her without her veil. "I don't think I'll ever stop telling you
how beautiful you are," he said with a smile. He stroked her hair and
kissed her forehead. "I feel really honoured to have you by my side... As
if I didn't deserve you because of the life I've led". Cynthia straightened
up to face him: "Don't say that! Even the companions of the Prophet
(salla Allahu 'alayhi wa salam) had a past before they converted to
Islam. I myself am not perfect and Allah doesn't ask us to be. Does He
not say that He is Forgiving? What counts are the people we are today

and the values that inspire us." And she added, "Never look at me as a perfect person but as someone who aspires to please Allah, with her faults and her qualities..." Liam laughed softly. "What are you laughing at?" Cynthia asked, puzzled. "You're the sweetest woman I've ever met. You're amazing...and you don't even know it." Cynthia smiled, "You'll be there to remind me then. May Allah allow us to grow old next to each other."

"Ameen" whispered the young man and he kissed her passionately. "I just want to look at you". Cynthia sat down to face him. "So do I." I've spent half my life looking down, I'm so happy to finally look up at a man and check him out as much as I want! And it's all halal! » They laughed. « Yeah, now I'm all yours » Liam said as he ran his hand through Cynthia's hair again, caressed her face and lingered on her lips. He seemed fascinated, knowing that he could now see her as she was, touch her, smell her sweet perfume.

The young woman also let herself be discovered by her husband. "Your eyes are hazel with touches of green! It's original. "I'm glad you think I'm original..." he said wryly. "And I love your lips" Cynthia said, caressing them with her fingertips. « Do you want a massage ? I'm pretty good at that» said Liam. « Let's see ! »

Cynthia turned her back to him. Liam began to undress her, helping her to remove her T-shirt. The young woman was wearing a cotton bra. Suddenly she felt embarassed. « Don't be shy or uncomfortable in front of me, you're beautiful." Liam whispered to her. She felt his hands gently press her shoulders, his fingers roving over her skin, down and up her back, lingering on the nape of her neck. It was really nice and felt good. He knew how to use his hands. And find her points of tension. After a few minutes she felt more relaxed

"We'd better get some rest, otherwise I don't think I'll be able to behave myself." Liam said. He kissed her neck.

They spent the rest of the night talking and after they'd changed, then fell asleep. The next day, Cynthia went into the kitchen to find

Liam baking her pancakes, he'd made a fruit salad and a courier had brought back some "pains aux chocolat" and croissants. "Next time I'll make you some myself insha'Allah," Cynthia told him. The whole day had just been wonderful. That evening, the two of them went down to the beach for dinner. They had long talks as if they had known each other all their lives. Cynthia was happy to feel that way. She knew it was something precious, something to be cherished. They were both sitting on a thick blanket and Liam had put down some cushions to make them comfortable. They had ordered dinner, which had been brought to them by courier. Sometimes Liam would say to her "Taste this, it's yummy! Masha Allah" and put a piece of meat or food in her mouth. "It's soo good! I like it!" After eating, they settled comfortably on the cushions next to each other. "You know, there's a hadith that I really like about soulmates. I love how it is described in Islam." "Me too," replied Liam. "The idea that we might have known each other when we were just souls and that that's what makes us so close... And that we'll find ourselves together again on Earth...It makes sense" Their bond was such that they were already anticipating what the other was going to do or say. Liam had got to know Cynthia first by observing her. He knew when she was sad, pensive, indecisive... He could read and feel all her emotions as if she were an open book. Cynthia felt the same way. "Normally now, you're supposed to be describing to me the types of stars in the sky...Like in the movies" "Yes, so cheesy" and they laughed. Liam said, "I don't know anything about stars, except that Allah has granted me one." Cynthia straightened slightly to look at her husband with a smile. "Oh, Allah granted you one?" "Yes, she's standing right next to me," Liam told her. "What a smooth talker!"

"Yes, but I think it's working Alhamdulillah" They kissed. "Speaking of cheesy...your little sister told me that you like romance novels, especially one of them..." "...Gone by the love" Replied Cynthia, thinking about how she would get even with Eve when she saw her... She also thought that now this book would seem totally different to her, now that she was living her own love story. To quote Solena, I've found my own Franco! The new couple stood up and moved off. Coordinated, they threw the paper plates into the bin bags they had brought with them. Then they collected the blankets and cushions. Before returning to their new home.

Tonight, Cynthia decided she was ready to share more with her husband. Outside, you could hear the waves crashing against the rocks. She had put on a satin nightdress and a satin lounge kimono, still shy and uncomfortable about showing herself fully to Liam. It was her first night, the first man she was going to spend the night with. She looked at herself in the mirror. She was happy and nervous at the same time. Happy to give herself to the man she loved and nervous about him seeing her body. She felt beautiful and vulnerable at the same time. After all, he'd undoubtedly been with women with experience and far more beautiful and voluptuous than her...like Hannah. "Yes, but he married you", she says to herself to give herself courage. When she entered the room, Liam looked at her intensely as if he were seeing her for the first time. He discovered her again. He finally saw the woman who was now his. "You're really beautiful Masha Allah." Liam said he was sitting on the bed. Shirtless and wearing a lounge jogger. The room was bathed in a soft, subdued light. Cynthia watched the man she loved, who was now her husband, approach her. He was undressing her with his eyes. « I don't have any experience... Can you teach me? » She said. "Yes. I'll teach you and you'll teach me to love you the way you want. We're husband and wife, we'll have plenty of time to learn to love each other. After all we've been through, I'm happy to finally be able to be with you, Cynthia.» Caressing her neck with his lips, he added « and...I've loved and wanted you since the first day I saw you..." She felt his hands run up her arms and stop on her shoulders. Gently, with his fingertips, he removed the satin kimono, which slid down to her ankles, and under his ardent kisses, Cynthia felt her body inflame with desire...he lifted her in his strong arms, brought her to the huge bed, and laid her down gently. With gentleness and patience, he took his time, introducing her to sensations that was completly new to her. Liam put an end to all her apprehensions and put her at ease. The young woman's heart was beating wildly and she could feel Liam's too. She held on to him as if she had waited for him all her life and she felt the same passion coming from her husband, the same need to be one. Nothing now stood between them and the love they felt. They was passionate, completely abandonned to each other. This was how Cynthia had imagined her first time. And she had no regrets about having waited so long, about having put up with remarks about the choices she had made to preserve herself until marriage and her way of life. She could feel a delightful sensation coursing through every inch of her body. It wasn't a question of virginity, but of offering herself to the right person. Samuel had said to her *"You'll never know love if you hold back all the time"*. Not only had she held back, but she was now living a love story. She was sharing this intimate moment with someone she trusted completely and who had married her and with whom she shared love. Nothing frightened her about Liam.

Fews days later

"Why did you want us to come back here for our Honeymoon?" Hand in hand, Cynthia walked with Liam. They were having a wonderful time and continuing to enjoy it. She loved him so much and knew that the feeling was mutual. She was grateful to Allah to answered to her duas and gave to her a wonderful husband. She was happy and peaceful. Her bare feet sank into the warm sand. The landscape around them was almost heavenly. The young woman then remembered the dream she used to have before getting married. "I wanted us to come back here because this is where it all began."

Chapter 20

EPILOGUE

"Gone With the Wind" was translated into dozens of languages. The author, a 15-year-old girl living in Paris, saw the rights to her work bought by Bollywood and Turkish studios.

To this day , a film has been released on Netflix in 3 parts. A 500-episode series with the characters of Antonio, the rich bad boy heir, Franco, the kindly farmer, and the young, pretty, and innocent (of course), fresh and delicate as a rose, Astafara, is currently running in Bollywood, Turkey and Mexico. When the young author was asked what inspired her to write her story during a live chat on Tiktok she replied:"I was really inspired by my big sister... And she added with a wink, "A hopeless romantic."

Chapter 21

« My heart is still broken but I found peace in faith and baking » had posted a picture of a cake on his Instagram page.

#boyscrytoo   #firstlove   #bakerman   #singlelifesuck #lookingfortheloveofmylife

@Thegirlnextdoor « Too bad, she don't know your value ! »

@Skyofloove : « I'm here for you if you need to speak, I know how you feel, I'm a heartbroken too ! »

@Deepestoftrue : « If my future man don't do that, i don't want it ! »

@Hannahqueen : « Pathetic! Obviously a delulu effect... »

@xxxOnlypan : « Check my profile »

@Pureheartandfaith : « May Allah facilitate you brother. May Allah send you a good sister, ameen »

@Ahmed33020 : « BrUUv !Y'all know that it was not your first try ! »

After Cynthia dumped him in front of his follower, Samuel start to become notorious. Right after, he received so many messages lot from women asking for him to marry them...The video became viral and he decided to exploit this new celebrity.

Surprisingly, he gained an impressive number of subscribers, always posting recipes, and it wasn't long before he was also offering live pastry classes. With a channel, a YouTube channel and a website, his popularity continued to soar, especially among women, who had rallied around him since his story with Cynthia. He was even welcomed on the set of « The Red flag » from Kimberly Show.

"We are here today with Samuel. A young man full of ambition and talent, a pastry chef. We've all seen that viral video where he proposed to the woman of his dreams... and was coldly rejected. Tell us a bit about that...What was your state, your reaction when she said no to you?"

"It was like a cold shower, Kimberley... My heart felt like it was the day I died..."

The presenter looked at the audience with an air of pity before returning her gaze to the young man.

"Here's a woman who doesn't know what she wants. You said in response to a comment on your instagram page, and I quote : "You travelled miles, bought a ring, so you thought she loved you?", your response: "She never told me otherwise. I was manipulated a little". "Did you feel you were manipulated Samuel?"

"I can say that yes, Kimberly, a cruel game of cat and mouse. People hide behind appearances, I'd say" Samuel looked at the main camera

"But I'm a forgiving man, I learn from my mistakes, in fact I've launched a mini coaching course for guys like me". And looking at the main camera "...and women who want to find love".

He added, biting his lips sensuously. "All you have to do is slip me a DM for any subscription," he said with a big, devastating smile and a mischievous look on his face... "You'll get a discount special."

"Is he for real? Honestly, you haven't missed a thing". Phew! The answers there were personal, you're officially the most hated girl on the Internet" declared Solena. Settled on the sofa, nibbling and sipping juice at Miriam's, the 3 girls had decided to get together for the holidays. They couldn't believe what they'd just witnessed.

"So...Do you want to watch The Search for Happiness? "NO!"

160

Chapter 22

"Call on Me; I will answer your prayers"

"Truly distress has seized me, but You are the Most Merciful of those who are merciful.' Then We heard his prayer and removed the distress that was on him, and We restored his people to him and doubled their number, a mercy from Us and a reminder to the worshippers." (**Surah Al Anbiya,21, Verse 83**)

Kassandra was seated at a table. It was going to be a long day. She was reviewing several sheets of paper on which she had written notes. She was served a refreshment by a lady. She readjusted her hijab. Not just any hijab, but one she design. Kassandra had launched her own modest wear brand and it was a big hit. On her Instagram page, she posted pictures of herself either in her luxurious New York flat, or in paradisiacal places, and always with a quote with a profound meaning. "Never forget who you are. Know that Allah is with you #myhijabmyreligion". Suddenly, a sister beckoned Kassandra to get ready. She picked up the sheets that the young woman had been reading. Suddenly Kassandra's clear voice was heard over the microphone. "Please take a seat". Today was her first conference and she was very proud of herself for all she had achieved, but above all because she was now fully practising and embracing her religion. When you entered the room, a large sign read: My conversion to Islam, overcoming the difficulties. Speaker: Kassandra, author of the books "Islam my happiness" "O richness, O sadness" Founder of the brand: « Beyourselfhijab »

Solena crossed the street, each of her hands holding that of a child. She had promised them that they would stop at Couronnes to buy books. The street was packed, with people sitting in the warmth of the sun on café terraces, while in a street lined with abaya shops and bookshops, people were doing their shopping. Solena went into the first bookshop that came along. While her children shopped, she wandered the aisles herself. At the checkout, she called Miriam, who had asked her for a specific name. But she couldn't find it: "Yes, it's Solena...". The brother set about putting his purchases in the bags. When she hung up, he asked her "Salam alaykum, Solena? From Paris?" She looked at him surprisedly. "Wow, how does he know a bout me??" "Yes, how did you know?" "Were you on Myhalallove?" Now, he had her full attention. "Why?" Solena asked. "We spoke a year ago but you blocked me..." The young woman immediately remembered him because she hadn't spoken to many men on this app. The only one who had really made an impression on her was a brother, whose profile she'd really liked and with whom she'd had a good chat, but who asked too many questions about her children. It had held her back. She tells him. "Sorry, I didn't mean to frighten you. As we talked about meeting, I wanted to give some presents to your children. I also work in an association that helps families in difficulty or isolated sisters with children. We often have toys, clothes, or passes for amusement parks. "He's not bad- looking either," Solena mused. "And you remembered me?" she said with a smile. Behind her, an elderly woman began to clear her throat, showing her impatience. "Yes as we got on so well?" "Listen Brother marry her, and pass on my articles!" Said the old lady. They both laughed. The brother asked Solena to wait. When the lady left, Solena returned to the checkout, and the brother insisted on offering her one of the books she had bought. She finally agreed. "Do you still want to get married insha Allah?" asked the brother. He asked her without looking at her, concentrating on the books he was putting in the bag. "Yes insha Allah and you?" "Still the case Alhamdulillah. When you blocked me, I left the app on for a while and then took it off. Solena felt embarrassed. "Sorry again." "That's fine Alhamdulillah. It doesn't matter. Qadr Allah. On the other hand...Would you accept a meeting with your wali?" "Yes, with pleasure insha Allah" Smiling, Solena added: "Qadr Allah".

AUTHOR NOTE

I dedicated this book to all my single sisters.

You will find your soulmate insha Allah. Don't be ever defeated or discouraged. Because Allah what we don't know. Everything is written Alhamdulillah.

Your sister fi Allah Marianne.

About the Author

Marianne Diatta is mom of 4 children. She is French and living in Uk. Business owner, and writer "Forget Wattpad ,love stories exist in real life is her first English novel.

To know more, follow her on: @mariannedwriter

Read more at https://www.thefrenchboudoirbeautybox.co.uk.

Milton Keynes UK
Ingram Content Group UK Ltd.
UKHW010841190424
441445UK00001B/45